1

Peoples' Servant
&
Resemblance

By
Bagher Mohama

INTRODUCTION

There are two stories in this book. The first one (Peoples' Servant) is pure fiction and the second one (Resemblance) is fiction based on a true event. Although the first story is about a king and his two sons (with completely different characters), alongside some adventures and romance but; the main purpose of writing this book is debate about the democracy, freedom of human, social justice and function of an ideal government. It challenges the readers, by looking at these issues rather differently; particularly in relation to the freedom as opposed to extreme liberalism, social justice and also being at the service of people. Also without entering too much in politics; disgraceful role of the superpowers, in causing misery to vulnerable nations is referred to, albeit briefly.

The second one is a short story about a baby who was snatched from his cot while mother and grandma were on vacation with their few months old child. What happens next is rather difficult to believe and yet, the central part of it is true. Of course, description of most of the scenes had to be imaginary; as those who were present at the time of this crime (and knew how exactly the things happened), are no longer with us. Having said so, to protect the privacy of surviving members of the families; neither real names of the characters have been mentioned in this book, nor the precise locations. B. M.

PEOPLES' SERVANT

CHAPTER 1

It was early-afternoon of a very cold winter day, when the audience began pouring out of a university conference theatre and it appeared that everyone was talking about the outstanding lecture they had just received. Two young students were among them; one wearing ordinary cloth and the other elegantly dressed.

"Putting lecture aside, I must say that you are very chic today Alex. Are you going to see a bird?"

"No, but I am really embarrassed about it. Everyone was looking at me; I suppose asking the same question. I am obliged to go to a party that I don't like but have to. I did not want to miss this lecture and there was no time to go home and change. So, here we are I came with such a ridiculous appearance to a lecture."

"Not ridiculous, just chic. All girls were looking at you because you are even more pretty today."

"Don't be silly. But before the party I must withdraw some money from this bank over there and pass it to a family near your place."

"So I better come in with you, we could walk together afterwards."

"Thank you that would be nice." They entered into the bank and Alex showed a cheque to the banker. He looked at them with obvious surprise and concern on his face.

"It is not safe to carry so much money with you sir." he said.

"Don't worry I have a body guard with me but please don't make it too bulky. Could it be all from the high value notes?" He got the money in two parts and put in his inside pockets.

The banker once again warned him of the danger of carrying so much cash.   As they turned towards the front exit, a middle aged man approached Alex and said, "I trust you must be Mr Alex Forman."

"Yes I am what can I do for you?"

"May I have a private word with you?"

"I have nothing to hide from my friend you can go ahead."

"Well sir, I am an intelligence officer," he showed his ID card and continued, "I have been sent to protect you Mr Forman."

"Is that so? Protect of what?

"There is a plot to assassinate you when you go out of the bank."

"Why someone should bother to assassinate a student?"

"I don't know the details but, General Trojan asked me early this morning, to find you and take you to the party that you have been invited."

"I was with General last night; he didn't say anything about it."

"Apparently the intelligence was received this morning."

"Sorry sir, I don't believe it and I cannot trust you. Please allow us to pass."   The intelligence officer took a sealed envelope from his briefcase and, while was passing it to Alex said, "It is interesting to see that General was absolutely right. He knew that you would not trust, so he wrote this hand written note to introduce me." Alex read the note inside the envelope and, having recognised hand writing of General Trojan said, "Well what you want me to do now."

"Don't trust him Alex," whispered his friend, "let us go."

"I don't trust him either but, I trust the General who has trusted him," Alex also whispered in return and continued, "Do not worry."

"I suggest we use that side door there," answered the officer "I have already parked my car behind it and two of my officers are watching to make sure all is clear. As far as we know sir, the assassins are waiting for you at the other side of building, but you never know, they might have intelligence too and change their place."

"You better come with us," said Alex to his friend, "I fear they might take you by mistake. We need to go towards your home anyway, to deliver this money."

"That is an excellent idea," said the officer confidently, "Mr Forman would sit on the back seat between two of my officers as a precaution and you sit beside me in front." They went out and did as they were told.   Alex showed the way towards his friend's house and when they got there the officer stopped the car to let his front seat passenger to leave.

"See you on Monday Alex and" he hesitated for a few seconds and continued "take care of yourself."

"Sure, good bye for now." Alex replied and noticed that his friend was making note of the car's number.

"Your friend does not trust me," said the officer, "he is making some notes."

"He is always suspicious, don't be offended."

When they were close to where Alex wanted to deliver the money he said, "Please stop the car just behind that red van." But the driver continued driving. "You passed it, please stop." He did not. And Alex said, "Well you need to turn back now."

"We don't have time for that." Officer replied.

"It is not important if I'm late for the party; please turn back I must deliver this money. In any case this is not the way leading to the place where I am invited to."

"We are not going there."

"Where are we going then, officer?"

"You will soon see it."

"You are after the money let me out immediately." Alex shouted but the officer once again ignored him. Now he became very concerned and began to struggle, trying to get out of the car and shouting, "Please stop the car".

"We are not after your money," said the officer, "we are employees of the government and are doing what we have been ordered." Alex stopped struggling momentarily in order to hear more but officer said no more.

"What have you been ordered to do?" asked Alex now extremely worried. But, there was no answer.

"Where are you taking me?"

"Be patient, I told you; you will soon see." Once again Alex started fighting with the guards pushing them towards the door and shouting "Stop it please, stop the car."

"Can you not control a child?" shouted the officer, "use that hand cuff and if needed tie his feet too. Just shut that boy up, I want to concentrate on driving." They did as they were told and Alex realised that he was truly in a very serious situation. He was now hand cuffed and tightly held between two guards. So, he stopped hopeless struggling and said, "I'm sure there is a mistake here. You have mistaking me with someone else."

"No we have not. Your pretty photo has been shown to me. Your full name is in my order. You've already confirmed your name. What else do you want Mr?" Alex was bitterly confused and speechless. "What is going on," he asked inside" why General Trojan has trusted him?" After about half an hour of driving they entered into a gigantic jungle and after another ten minutes' drive, they stopped beside a waterfall. It was a beautiful place to be even in the bitter cold weather.

"You see what a beautiful place we have chosen for you?" The officer said cheerfully.

"Why are we here?"

"To help you to do what you've requested yourself. Pardon me, not requesting but written yourself." The cool officer answered and began fastening a long and strong rope on the trunk of a tree.

"What are you doing?"

"Don't you remember the letter sir?" said the officer while bringing an envelope out of his pocket. Then he carefully opened the envelope and showed the letter inside of it to shocked and confused Alex "Here is your own hand written letter, explaining why you are commuting suicide."

"Committing suicide?" cried Alex and read the letter that was his own hand writing. "This is my hand writing but I have not written it. Please listen to me; there is conspiracy here.   This is a fake letter and I have no doubt General's is forgery too. Someone has tricked you. Do not involve yourselves in this horrible crime. All you need to do is to get in touch with General Trojan; he will confirm that, the letter is not from him and he has not heard anything about the assassination plot."   One of the guards, rather older than the other said, "Perhaps he is right, let us call the General."

"Shut up." Shouted his boss "The official instructions and the information that I have been given, leave no doubt in my mind that we should do what we have been ordered to do. Get on with the job now, it is very cold I can't stand here and argue with you fools. He is a threat to national security as I've been told and all the evidence confirms it. Do you want to serve your country and king or not? Do you realise what could happen to us if you disobey?" He put the letter in Alex's pocket and said, "Get on with job now." They began to push Alex towards the edge of valley in order to put the already made loop of the rope around his neck.   He cried and desperately pleaded, "Don't do this please. You are making a big mistake I'm not a threat to national security. This ridiculous accusation is part of a conspiracy. I assure you General does not know anything about it and he will kill you all if you do such a crime."

"Don't waste my time," said the officer "Get on with the job I said." He then went into the car and lighted a cigarette. He noticed the two men and Alex are still talking but did not hear them. He pulled the window down and shouted at them, "You fool; are you going to hang this boy with hand cuff on.   Who could commit suicide with his hands tied on his back? Take it off; make it natural."   They did so and officer pulled the window up and poured a cup of tea for himself from flask beside him. He noticed one of the men helping Alex to put his gloves on and said to himself "Not a bad idea at all. He wouldn't have come here without having his glove with him. It is too cold even for someone who is about to commit suicide." He also noticed they are very gently dropping him into the valley while cord is around his neck. "They are too kind to the boy, I don't blame them. I feel sorry for him too but what can I do? General says he is a threat to the country and my duties to king and country come first."

When the hangmen finished hanging Alex and began walking towards the car with evident depressed faces, the officer got out of the car and said, "Look at this beautiful scene. I want a photo from here." He gave a camera to one of the men and said "Take a good picture from me and that waterfall," and he showed him how to operate it, "I will stand on the edge of valley and you make sure that, waterfall is in the frame too." Once it was done he said, "Now I will take a picture from both of you together. Please stand where I was standing, as far as possible near to the edge. Make sure you are not obstructing the waterfall. Yes that is good, a bit closer together. That is fantastic. Don't move anymore." He then took out a gun from his pocket and shot them both with no feeling. They fell into the valley. He came closer to the edge and made sure that they are both dead. He looked around and then went into the car and drove at the same route that he had entered the jungle.

"I am sorry for them," he said inside, "but when it comes to national security and guarding our king nothing else matters. I've done exactly what I was ordered to do." He was not sure about his self-reassurance, "Oh God," he added, "please forgive me."

CHAPTER 2

Alex did not die. He was of course frightened to death and cried terribly loud while falling into valley but as he was descending; by following exact instructions that he had received, he managed to pull the loop of the rope away from his neck just in time before being strangled by. It caught the side of his neck and caused laceration which was very sore in the cold weather. He was shivering both from cold and fear. He dropped the loop and pulled himself up the rope to make sure it is near his feet and used the loop as a step to stand on it and remained silent. He was indeed in a very odd situation; being extremely scared, concerned about his parents and friend, suffering from harsh cold as well as pain on his right shoulder and hand but at the same time; admiring the beauty of the place; tall trees, the magnificent waterfall above his head and the river under his feet with their harmonious music. When he heard that the officer shot both of his colleagues, he was even more frightened and prayed that the murderer would not find out that his victim had not died with broken neck. Therefore, his fear and shivering increased and he was worried that because of shivering, the movement of the rope will alert the officer to check the situation more closely. He put his head close to the rope somehow to pretend that he was strangled in the loop. Then he heard the car leaving the area and immediately began to pull himself up the rope. When he reached near the edge of valley he was so tired that could not hold the rope tight enough. He alternated using his hands in holding the rope in order to give temporary rest to them and then started climbing up again. When he reached the edge of valley he could not grip the rope further up because it was pulled very firm due to his weight and fixed on wall of valley; leaving no gap to push his hand or finger through it.   So he held the upper part of rope with one hand and with the other hand; hurled it round his waist and hips several times, until it was shortened enough to reach the loop and put his feet on it again. With such a clever idea and tactic; Alex was able to stand and rest on that useful loop, but of course, at the expense of extreme pain on his abdomen and back. However this gave him a desired confidence; to take his hands off the rope and start grasping the stones, roots of the trees, plants and whatever he could find on the wall, in order to crawl upward and sideward. Few minutes later he reached the flat ground and fell listless on the freezing surface covered by snow, totally worn out both mentally and physically. His trousers were dirty and had many cuts and tears but his jacket was less dirty and hardly damaged. It was getting a bit dark and snow had begun to fall again. He realised that he could not afford to stay there any longer or worse still to fall asleep there. Although he had aches and pains on his arms and hands but his feet were strong and fresh to run. So he took the track of the car and said inside, "Surely this path will take me out of this scary jungle." He remembered that, from the time car had entered into the jungle it took about ten minutes to get that place but obviously it would take him a bit longer on foot, even though he was running fast. Strong wind striking the icy snow on his face and dark passage between the trees had created a scary and uncomfortable surrounding and situation. When he was tired he rested a couple of minutes and took the opportunity to empty his bladder.   After which he continued running, while both snowing and his tiredness was increasing.   His fragile hopes of reaching to road and finding help were declining fast when he suddenly beheld a road in front of him, "I'm out of jungle," he cried loudly "thank God." He rushed forward as he had heard a car approaching and hurriedly waved his hands to stop it but the car passed him.   Hope gave him a new energy and he run after the car and shouted "Save me, save me." After a minute or so car stopped and reversed towards him.   A young couple in rear seat were looking at him from behind the window half way pulled down. He shouted, "I'm a student, help me please. They wanted to kill me." The young lady told the driver to open the front door and Alex hastily jumped in. The driver looked at his appearance with suspicion.   Alex said, "Thank you. My name is Alex Forman. I am student of Maxim University. Please take me somewhere that I can take a taxi."

"There is no taxi around here and the roads would close shortly, I am sure," said the young lady, "we will find somewhere for you to stay tonight. You need drink, please take this cup of tea." She poured tea from flask into a disposable cup and handed it to Alex. He thanked and drunk it hurriedly.

"Shortly after I had left the conference hall, they kidnapped and brought me to jungle there and hanged me."

"Oh my God," cried the lady, "but why?" and after a pause added, "How dreadful. Thank God you are okay."

"I don't know why."

"We attend the same University," said the young man "I am in the medical school and my sister is in faculty of art. Which college are you?"

"I am postgraduate student of law."

"I think I have seen you."

"I play basketball;" said Alex with low voice almost asleep "probably you have seen me in the matches."

"Yes, I now remember, you are captain of the team."

"Yes." After this yes, Alex fell sleep. He was indeed worn out.

"We must take him home," said the young lady, "it is very cold weather and I cannot think of anywhere else."

"Your father will not like it," said the driver "in fact he will be mad with you, I warn you."

"What do you suggest? Leaving him on the road to freeze?"

"I know your father better; he will never allow a stranger in his house. He doesn't trust the strangers I'm sure. That is all I am telling you."   They arrived home which was a magnificent mansion. The car entered into big courtyard and stopped in front of stony staircase.   Driver took the car to garage and three of them walked up stairs, Alex with some difficulty as he had just woken up.   When they reached to entrance door which was well lighted, the young lady and her brother noticed the muddy appearance of poor Alex with all cuts and tears on his clothes.

"Oh my God," said the sister, "you are wounded. I will ask my mother to do something about it; she used to be a nurse."

"It isn't much I just could not remove loop of the rope quickly enough.   It must be a bit of scratch." By then an old female servant had opened the door.   Alex looked at the marbled and shiny corridor and said, "I cannot come in with these dirty shoes, I cannot get them out either.   My feet are frozen; could you please give me two carrier bags?"   The couple went in and soon the bags were brought and he put his feet in each of bags and tied them on his leg.   He then entered and immediately took off his gloves and began warming his hands on the hot radiator and said, "Thank you. Could you please give me a pillow and a blanket; I will sleep here."

"No, please do come in," said the brother "here will be too cold when the central heating is off."   Now Alex truly looked ridiculous; with muddy and torn trousers, an elegant jacket albeit covered with some dirt, clean and stylish waistcoat underneath it, white shirt and a bow tie while his feet were in two carrier bags. His face had a few dirty spots on it and hair was messy and muddy. Brother and sister walked in front and Alex with the assistance of old servant followed behind.   They entered the reception room where their parents, four guests, amongst them two old ladies, and their younger sister were waiting.

"We were very worried about you," said the father, "you are late." At this point he noticed the stranger and said, "What is this?"

"He is a student," said his daughter, "we brought him to stay with us tonight. There is no transport to take him home." "Is he a student with that elegant cloth and a bow tie?" said father, "Elegant but of course covered with dirt. Who are you?"

"He is in the same University we go," said his daughter, "He says they kidnapped him and, brought to jungle to hang."

"I see, and you believed him."

"Yes, there is a sign on his neck. Mother could you look at it please?"

"Don't approach him," shouted the husband to his wife who was coming closer to examine stranger's neck, "he is a criminal, member of drug gang or something.   This is the rivalry and fighting between the gangs. We don't want to get involved. Get out sir."

"Father, he is student," said his son, "he can show his ID card."

"Of course," said father, "they need someone to distribute drugs in University too." At this moment the butler arrived to serve. "Put it on table for the time being," said his boss, "search that boy.   Alex attempted to take his ID card from his pocket but angry father shouted, "Don't move" and took out his gun, "hold your hands up. "And turning to butler said, "Be careful I think he has gun inside his jacket. I can see the bulging there." Alex said, "It is not a gun" and tried to reach to his pocket again to show the money, "it is...." but once again boss shouted, "Don't move, I will shoot if you do."   The rest of people in the room were very frightened particularly young daughter who started weeping and said, "Don't shoot him please, don't do it please." The butler searched but did not find a gun. Instead, he took both packs of the money out and showed to his boss and said, "Very big notes sir."

"What did I say? He is member of a gang. Have you seen so much money in a student's pocket?   That is dirty money. That is what the gangs fight for. Put it back and throw him out. Move or I will shoot."

"That is not dirty money sir," Alex began talking after another terrifying situation, "I got it from bank before I was kidnapped. I meant to give it to a family who urgently needs it before they are thrown out of their house on Monday."

"What a caring and generous criminal we have here," said the father sarcastically, "what a clever liar you are. Get out before I lose my temper more than I already have. Give this boy a blanket and show him the way out."

"No father," shouted his elder daughter and went towards Alex to shield him with her body ,while her father continued pointing at Alex with his gun, "he will freeze to death if you throw him out." At this point younger daughter joined her sister to help in shielding Alex and while still weeping said, "Don't shoot him. Don't throw him out please, he can use my room."

"Colonel, I beg you put that gun down," said one of the guests, "accidents can happen. Let us think calmly and see what should be done." Colonel obeyed the gest reluctantly.

"I see you are an officer so you must know General Trojan." Alex began to talk very much touched with the action of sisters. He was almost in tears.

"Everyone knows him, what about it?"

"He knows me and if you call him he will assure you that I am not criminal."

"You are lying again and you know I cannot get hold of him at this time of evening."

"You can call him at home, his number is," he gave the number," I am sure he is at home."

"How does he know you?" Colonel enquired.

"My father is his servant and my mother occasionally helps his wife."

"A butler's son with such elegant attire, are you really expecting me to believe you?"

"They've almost brought me up in their house and love me like their own children. I was supposed to go for a party and General wants me to be seen as a rich man's son. I don't like it at all but I have to obey him."

"Father let us call General please," said his daughter, "I think he is not lying but you could find out if he does by simply trying this number." She then asked the number again and dialled.

"Allo, is that General Trojan's house? Is it? Good. Please hold the line a gentleman wants to talk." She then passed the telephone to Alex who had taken a tissue from table nearby. He took the receiver using a tissue, as he had some mild lacerations on his finger tips and did not want to contaminate it.

"Allo is that Olan? This is Alex, is the boss at home? Okay, tell him I want to talk to him. Wait a minute Olan, tell him not to say a word and just listen to me. It is a matter of national security. Do you understand? Yes Olan that is what I said." He then waited while the rest of audience were curious and in absolute silence. Colonel seemed rather concerned but he still thought that Alex was playing a trick.

"Good evening. Please forgive me for asking you to listen and not to say a word. This is a matter of grave concern and as a result of what happened I couldn't go to party. I will explain later but first I need your assistance urgently. I'm in the house of a Colonel who thinks I am a criminal. I ask you to reassure him that I am not. I must rest here tonight but Colonel wants to throw me out. I will die in the freezing cold out there." As these words were spoken Colonel became even more worried. "I pass the telephone to Colonel now," continued Alex, "but later I will tell you what happened. Sir I've already told them that my father is your servant. Please just reassure him." He then passed the telephone to astonished and clearly nervous Colonel.

"Good evening sir this is Colonel Poxon sir. Yes Sir. Yes Sir. Yes sir same place. Yes sir, you honoured us few months ago. Yes sir, of course sir." After all of these yes sirs he seemed flushed and sweaty and with some respect returned the telephone to Alex. Colonel was in a dreadful state of mind and while anxiously looking at his wife sat on a chair in deep thoughts.

"Thank you sir I cannot go into the details over telephone but briefly; after I got the money from bank I was kidnapped, brought to a jungle not too far from this house and was hanged in the valley. I didn't die." Here he giggled and said "silly me, of course I did not die; how could I talk now if I had died? Anyway, after the car left I climbed the rope and later was rescued by Colonel's kind daughter and son. General, please don't tell anything about it to anyone including my parents. Whoever enquired about me the answer is that I forgot to go to the party; came to see a friend and I am staying with him over night. I am sure that they have mistaken me with someone who is very important to you and I don't want to name here. If the conspirators find out that, I am not dead; they will trace and find me here to kill. Because I am now a witness to their crime and I have seen documents that link the plot to very high authorities." After a pause and listening carefully Alex continued, "Yes sir, it is a mystery but I will clarify tomorrow. Please send your driver," but he cut the sentence and said; "hold the line please." He then politely enquired from the lady of the house what time is their breakfast on Saturdays and once he heard the reply, continued talking to General.   "Sorry sir, yes please send your driver tomorrow morning exactly at nine o'clock.   There are reasons for everything that I say now and all will be clear to you tomorrow. Sir, this must be a very rare occasion that you are in receiving end of the orders, please forgive me for that. There should be no calls to this house tonight and nobody should hear that I'm here. Tomorrow, if the driver got here early, he should wait until it is nine o'clock before ringing the bell and if there was any delay on the road he should call at nine to inform this house. There are forensic evidences in the crime scene which needs to be collected. So, we need a special team here who can do that. Some of the things are in the bottom of a very deep valley. Thank you for being patient with m and, good night. Wait sir, one more thing. You will remember our conversation last week. You are right this cannot go on." He listened again and said, "Yes sir, that is fine with me. Now I can say good night." He returned the receiver to relieved but astonished daughter of the Colonel.   Everyone else was speechless and in total silence.

"Sorry," said Alex, "conversation took a long time. I apologise from all of you."   He then turned to Colonel and said, "I take it that you will allow me to stay."

"Yes," answered Colonel, "sorry about my suspicion."

"Thank you sir," Alex said, "I have two more requests if you don't mind sir.   First request is this; please do not allow the news of you having a stranger in this house to get out. This is for the safety of your own family as well as mine for reasons you heard me telling to General. Second request is, please leave me alone with your children and kind helper for a few minutes."

Colonel without saying a word led his guests and wife to another room all seemed engaged in their thoughts trying to figure out; who this young stranger is and what General Trojan told to our poor host that changed him so dramatically and so suddenly.

"Now," said Alex with a sigh, "you've saved my life and caused trouble and headaches for yourselves. You'll feel it when I start asking for more help. I need to take shower and borrow some cloths from you doctor, if you allow me. I need a big carrier bag to put my dirty things in it, a pillow, linen and a blanket to sleep in a corner. You see what I mean by trouble?"

"No trouble, you can use my room," said older sister, "there is shower there."

"No, use mine," interrupt younger sister, "I said it first when father was trying to kill him."

"I cannot borrow cloths from you. I will go to doctor's room."

"You are welcome. There is a shower in my room too," said the brother, "but let me help you, I see you are exhausted and in pain."

"Yes doctor; I've pain in my legs, arms, shoulder, back, almost everywhere." Alex replied half-jokingly "But I'll be alright after shower and short rest." He began walking but stumbled, so he was held by brother in one side and the old servant at the other. Sisters watched them with pity evident on their faces.

"Poor young man, they really hanged him." said the older sister, "What a horrible thing to do. It is cruel and inhumane. Why they did it? They did not steal his money so they were not thieves. Who were they?"

"He said something to General," said younger sister, "a plot involving important people."

"Yes he did. He has seen documents about it."

"It will be in the papers in a few days' time."

"If influential people are behind it, we won't see it there."

"Father suddenly changed after talking to General, why?"

"General Trojan is the most senior officer in the Army. He has four stars on his shoulder. In fact he is the only one with four stars. He probably was angry with father because of what he was about to do. Now poor father is worried about his future promotions in Army. That is what bothers him I think."

"That must be. He hardly talked afterwards. Have you seen Alex at university?"

"No, but Ravid has seen. He is the captain of basketball team of his college."

"Perhaps the other teams plotted to kill him."

"Don't be silly, let us go and see what father is doing." Then they joined the rest of the family and guests. Everyone was busy talking about what had happened but no one had a clue. The old ladies were in agreement with the Colonel that Alex looked like a criminal but, could not understand his elegant attire and the manner of speech to General Trojan. One of the guests solved the problem; "With that sort of money you can buy anything and as for the way he talked, perhaps General has a hand in the business." Colonel dismissed it rather angrily, "He does not need dirty money. After his majesty the king he is the most important person in the country and is the most trustworthy officer in the army."

"Sorry Colonel; is it safe to have a gun with you while you are at home?" asked one of the ladies, "I don't know much about the gun of course."

"Yes it is safe," Colonel answered, "we are too far from the city and police protections. I keep it with me just in case there was a burglar or intruder." They then began talking about other matters and lady of the house went to attend the preparations for dinner.

CHAPTER 3

When Alex was brought to bedroom of the caring medical student, he obviously looked ill and fell on the sofa while thanking them and apologising for the trouble. "Doctor, "he said, "I hope you will not regret saving me."

"Please don't think so," said the brother, "but before anything else you need a warm drink. This is our kind housekeeper who will bring you a glass of hot milk perhaps with some honey in it?" The old housekeeper thought it was a good idea. When she turned to leave the room Alex said "Please do not forget other things I have asked for."   Few minutes later housekeeper came back alongside a young servant, who was carrying what Alex had requested.   Hot milk with honey and analgesic which brother had already given was very effective indeed and after the servants had left Alex said, "Doctor..," But medical student interrupted him. "My name is Ravid, I am not doctor yet."

"You will be. Okay Ravid, could I borrow trousers, jacket, shoes and socks please but all from the used ones. Please only the ones that you use at home."   Ravid gave what was asked for and added shirt and new underwear but Alex did not think he would need them.

"I leave there in case you need.   I will fill bath and you better rest in warm water for some time before you take shower."   He showed how shower works and where shampoo, soap etc. are and left him on his own. "I will come back in an hour or so," he said on leaving the room, "but don't rush."

By the time Ravid returned Alex had already changed and put his dirty trousers, jacket etc. in the bag. He had made sure that everything in the pockets were shifted to borrowed cloths and had decided not to use tie any more.

"Mum would like to examine your neck if you don't mind." He did not and so she came and examined.

"It is not too bad," she said, "fortunately laceration is not deep. Exposing to air would heal it faster but, before you go to bed I will put dressing bandage on it to make it a bit comfortable for you." Once mother had left Ravid said "This is your room for tonight Alex. There is an extra bed in Enzel's room I will sleep there.   Enzel is my younger sister. Please feel free to read any book you want, write if you wish, listen to radio or television. Just do whatever you would do in your own room."

"Thank you very much. I will sleep on this sofa. You can still use your own bed."

"It will not be comfortable on sofa."

"I am used to."

"I will leave the room for you anyway and I hope you will make yourself comfortable."

*

Housekeeper nocked the door and announced the dinner. Together, they went to the dining room where all had already taken their seats. Alex appeared clean and very handsome now. They showed his place beside the lady of house.   He looked at the smart dining table with its stylish arrangements and various dishes on it and said, "Sorry I cannot sit there. I will not be able to eat if I sit there. I am a very shy and clumsy person. I will take my plate, a spoon and a glass and sit on that table in the corner."   They insisted on him to sit with them but he too insisted not to by saying, "If you want me to be at ease, please allow me to sit where I can eat without breaking something." And he sat where he had pointed to.

"I will join you." said the younger sister who had brought her plate with her and sat beside him. Colonel was not happy at all but his wife made a sign advising him to relax and let the uninvited guest be served separately if that makes him more comfortable and happier. So, the servants served them separately and as they were eating, Alex began chatting with young girl.

"Thank you Enzel for joining me but I see your father is very angry with both of us."

"He is not. Who told you my name?"

"Your brother said but I believe you are an angle and that is what I should call you. When you cried for my ordeals and tried to protect me I was very much touched. I nearly cried. My friends say I am too sensitive; perhaps I am. "

"I was very sorry for you and that was why I cried. Father shouldn't have treated you like that. I am very crossed with him."

"Please don't say so. He was protecting his family. That is his responsibility He thought I was a criminal."

"You don't look like a criminal I think you look like a prince." "That's a very nice thing to say to a servant's son. No one has ever said such a kind word to me. You are really an angle. Isn't it strange that your father sees me a criminal and you see a prince and yet I'm the same person?"

"Criminals are ugly but you are very pretty that is why I didn't think you are criminal. My sister and brother did not agree with father either."

"Thank you, you are all very kind. But it is not correct to say criminals are ugly. There are many handsome men and very beautiful women, who are evils, criminals and do many wrong things. And equally there are ugly people who are very nice and kind and hardly do anything wrong. You can't judge the people with their look and whether or not they are pretty."

"I suppose you are right. Some of my friends are not pretty but they are very nice, polite and kind."

"That is why Colonel didn't take my appearance in consideration," he laughed and added, "supposing you are right about my face. By the way, I know your brother's name but what is your sister's?"

"Tophia, she is very beautiful, isn't she?"

"So are you. How old are you?"

"I am twelve next birthday."

"Do you want me to tell you how they hanged me and how I escaped?"

"Yes please."

*

After they had finished eating and drinking, Alex called one of the servants and asked if it is possible to find some string for him and asked Enzel if she had toy persons among her toys which she had and brought one.

"Three men had kidnapped me. The man in charge fastened the rope to trunk of a big tree as low as possible. It was fastened very low as I'm showing now;" Alex fastened the string to leg of the table lamp, "so that when rope was spread on the ground and was stretched towards the valley, it was touching the ground. The stone on the edge of valley was a bit higher than ground which means rope was tightly fixed on it. I can't show it on this table but remember that point because later on it became a big problem for me."

"I can imagine it." Enzel said.   She was too eager to hear the rest of the story and would have said so even if she did not follow the point.

"Anyway boss went into the car because he didn't want to stay in cold any longer. Two of his colleagues were just about to hang me, without listening to my desperate efforts to convince them that I am innocent. I made one more effort and reminded them that when this crime was discovered General Trojan will find and kill them.   One of them said, "I want to believe you but I cannot disobey the boss and in any case if we don't; he will come and hang you himself. But we will show you a way to escape after we have left."

"How?" asked Enzel no longer able to wait.

"Well, first he allowed me to wear the gloves and then he rotated the rope twice around my right hand and asked me to grasp the rope with same right hand, just above the small loops in it; like this." He showed what he means on the toy person. "This was to prevent rope to slip from my hand when I fall down. Then he put the big loop at the end of rope that was already prepared for hanging around my neck and said, "I have to do this to show the boss that we are hanging you.   But, as soon as we let you go take it off your neck and use it as a step down there and make no noise."   Alex showed this too on the toy and then described how he escaped but did not say anything about the fate of those unfortunate men.   "Now, as you can see when this toy man gets near the edge; there is no gap between rope and the wall or the ground above, to get hold of the rope in order to pull himself up a bit more and reach flat surface. And that was exactly what happened to me and I had to crawl side way"   He described how he did it and continued, "If they had fastened the rope in the middle of trunk; there would be an angle near the edge and I could simply jump and catch it."   He then fastened the cord in middle of the foot of imaginary tree to show Enzel what he means. He also described his running to find a help and his rescue by her sister and brother precisely when his feet were beginning to fail him and his hope was vanishing.

"You were very clever."

"Not clever enough. I could not take the loop off my neck in time. When they practically dropped me into the valley, the first few seconds was so horrifying that, I couldn't think of a loop around my neck and therefore there was a delay in taking off and that is the reason for scratch on my neck.   Your mother says it will soon heal if I leave it exposed to air."

"Is it very painful?"

"No doctor Ravid gave me pain killer, it is better now. In fact most of aches and pains are gone." After a pause Alex added, "But I think I have tired you too much. It is almost time for bed now." When Alex turned to see if the rest of people in dining room had finished their coffee he found Tophia standing behind him and softly said, "Oh, how long have you been here?"

"Sorry, I could not help but to come and listen to the story. I have been here since you put your gloves on." She laughed, "Please forgive me for being so nosey.   But everyone else was listening except that they did not come as close as I did because they are not as nosey as I am.   They kept their silence to hear you without coming so close.

"Angel, was I talking too laud? I am sorry it appears that I was," said Alex rather embarrassed and as he was rising added, "Anyway, I leave the rest of story to breakfast time. Angle; make sure everyone is there." He then walked towards the elders and thanked the lady of the house, apologised for disturbing them by his loud talk with Angel and politely said good night.

Ravid accompanied him and when they were in his room once again Alex announced, "I'll sleep on sofa or floor, you can use your own bed." And once again Ravid said no and added, "I have left some drink and biscuit on table. I will come at about eight o'clock so that we can go together for breakfast. As Ravid was about to leave mother nocked the door and came in.

"That was terrifying ordeal, how much you have suffered. I can't wait to hear the rest of the story but I hope it will be happier one. I have brought this wet gauze containing antiseptic to put on the scratch to prevent it getting infected and, I will cover with dry dressing bandage. Is that okay?" She did so and as she was leaving the room Alex said, "Many thanks. You are very kind. You are all kind people."

"I hope you will have a pleasant sleep and good rest." As Ravid was leaving Alex asked if the room has key. The answer was yes.

"Could you please lock the door from behind?" Alex requested.

"You can lock it from inside."

"No, I want you to do from outside. I think your father still is suspicious of me."

"I really do not think so," and then he thought perhaps Alex is concerned about his safety and with this excuse wants the room be locked so, he added, "Okay I will lock it and take the key with me. Good night."
"Good night and thank you" said Alex.

CHAPTER 4

Alex woke up at about seven o'clock. He took shower and then made certain preparations including writing a note. He folded the linen and blanket and put them on sofa and pillow on top of them. He also put the bag beside the door to remember to take with him later on. It was just after eight when he heard the door unlocked and Ravid entered after knocking the door.

"Good morning Alex. I hope you had a pleasant sleep and have recovered from aches and pains."

"Good morning. Yes, thanks to you and your mother. Dressing helped a lot and of course the analgesic you gave. I took the dressing off as mother advised and surely in few days' time it will heal completely."

"Are you ready for breakfast?"

"Yes."

They went together to dining room. It was exactly a quarter past eight and everyone was ready for the breakfast and perhaps more ready and eager to hear the rest of story. After they had finished having their breakfast, Alex thanked the Colonel and his wife, and said to Ravid, "I just pop in your room for one more time and get ready for the departure. But please don't disappear I have not finished the story yet." In coming back he brought the bag with him and called the housekeeper to the corridor behind the dining room and whispered "Thank you for your help please accept this." and he gave her some money. "No sir, this is too much." said the housekeeper. "It is not." said Alex, "please send someone to clean the bathroom and tidy the room." He took the bag towards the butler who was standing beside the window watching outside and said, "I leave this bag here for the time being, could you please put it in the car when they come to fetch me"?   He gave money to him too who like the housekeeper said it was too much but accepted with thanks.   "Please could you find your driver and ask him to get the car ready he must show us the way to waterfall."   He then returned to the table, took off a chain with a medallion attached to it from his neck and began cleaning and shining it with tissue.

"Well Enzel, last night I said you are an angel and I still stand by my word.   I will never forget your tears. An angel cried for the suffering of a poor man like me.   Back to story now; yesterday certain wicked persons wanted to see me dead.   Their plan was that when my body was found hanging down the valley the police will find a note in my pocket and conclude that I have committed suicide and left a letter with my own handwriting to explain why I did. Can you believe it? I saw that letter. It was my own handwriting but I had not written it. For some reason they didn't want to shoot me by gun or kill with a knife. They wanted it to be seen and reported as another suicide. They hanged me down the valley and left me to die there but God had another plan." He looked at the clock it was about fifteen minutes to nine.   "God wanted me to live a bit longer and meet good people like you, your sister, brother and mother in order to realise; how important it is to help and support, when a fellow human needs it. God wanted me to experience it firsthand so that if one day I was in a position to help, I do so. And here in this house I promise I will help. Remember that."   He looked at clock again and showed the chain and medallion to Enzel, "This is made from 24 carat gold. On one side of it you see the sign of cross and the word of Jesus and on the other side it is written Allah.   That is what the Muslims call God.   I have both on the medallion because I believe there is only one God but in every language or religion a different name is used to address him or refer to. Here under Allah there are few lines from Quran. Apparently it would protect you from danger if you've it with you. But I don't believe in it and I don't think this had a role in saving me yesterday."

At this point Alex put the chain around Enzel's neck and said, "You'll make me very happy if you accept this as a present."

"Oh that is beautiful," said Enzel while showing it to her mother with joy "thank you very much."

"You are welcome angel. But it is not something that you should wear for school. Perhaps mum could keep it for you and when you are older, you can show to your friends and say this is my present from a prince."

"Are you a prince?" Enzel shouted with mixture of surprize and happiness.

"Well, last night you said that I looked like a prince. Are taking it back? Are you?"

"No. I am not taking back" Alex took off a ring and began cleaning with another tissue and said; "General's wife spoils me. Last year I saw this ring and said what a beautiful ring. She immediately took it off her finger and gave it to me. I said no Madam I can't have it, that is for ladies. She said; keep it with you. One day you will see a lady who deserves to have it." Then Alex presented it to Tophia and said, "Would you accept this as present?"

"No I cannot, that is too expensive. But thank you for offering."

"I knew it; how can one expect Colonel's daughter to accept present from a servant's son."

"Please don't say so, that is not the reason. It is just too expensive thing for a present."

"Okay, please wear it for a few minutes it will not hurt you. You could return it when I am inside the car; if you felt it's not insulting to refuse a present." Tophia did so and Alex said, "It is even more beautiful on your finger." It appeared everyone was fascinated, hypnotized or perhaps just trapped in the story. No one was talking and Colonel seemed lost in his thoughts, struggling with the worries which he had developed since talking to General the night before. Alex took off his gold Rolex watch from his wrist and once again began cleaning it while talking to Ravid, "I've no idea why twenty first birth-days should be so important for the families. In mine, General regarded it a special birthday and gave this as a present," here he smiled at Tophia and said, "and I didn't refuse it. However I think it is more fitting to a doctor's wrist than mine. I wonder if you would kindly accept it from me."

"What are you doing?" Colonel shouted. He was not happy with what he was hearing and seeing and, at this point he could no longer control himself. "Do you realise that it worth ten thousand dollars? Who are you sir? You are not a servant's son. You have not told me the truth." He was now very angry.

"As for who am I," Alex reached to his pocket to get his ID card out "This is my name sir; Alex Forman. You did not allow me to show it last night. As for the price of watch it is not ten but twenty thousand. You think my life does not worth that much, is that what you think? They've saved my life. How much would you be prepared to pay to save your son's life?" Since arrival to that house this was the first time that Alex had lost his temper but he instantly calmed himself down. Until then Colonel had thought that Alex was General Trojan's son but they didn't want him to know. There was something in the voice of General that had given this impression to Colonel. Now that he had seen the ID, this could no longer be the case which made him even more anxious and perplexed. His gut feeling was telling him that it is not as simple as Alex trying to show; there is something mys-terious in the business. The rest of the audience were totally mystified with the story and extraordinary generosity of their uninvited guest. They asked themselves why he is giving away tens of thousands so easily. Who is he that dares to talk like that with Colonel? However, after that interruption Alex pre-sented the watch to Ravid.

"No Alex, that is really too much I cannot possibly accept."

"You can't accept for the same reason as your sister, sorry I keep forgetting my status. But allow me to see it on your wrist. You can return it when your sister does." He looked at the clock again it was two minutes to nine. He then stood up and said,

"It is almost time to say good bye." He bent towards Enzel and said, "May I hug you please?" he did so and kissed her forehead. "Good bye angel." He raised himself, went towards Tophia and said, "Lady Tophia, I cannot find a meaningful word to express my gratitude to you. I have to use the same word that everyone else does; thank you very much."   He shook her hand, kissed it politely and gave her a small piece of paper and added, "This is short note for you, please read it after I have gone." Tophia blushed and took it with shaky hand and remained speechless. After that farewell he said, "Thank you Ravid." and hugged him "I will keep these as souvenirs, unless you wanted me to return to you?"

"Don't make me embarrassed Alex. They are nothing to be returned."

"For me they are precious.   Ravid, you will be an excellent doctor and our nation will be very proud of you."

It was exactly nine when the bell rang. Butler looked from the window and after a minute said, "Sir, an army truck entered and a car, and another car and another truck." Colonel rose to his feet clearly agitated. "What?" he said while rushing towards the window.

"Your house is now invaded but don't worry sir, they will not cause any harm," said Alex, "you know this General; he is master of show off." He then said "Good bye Madam, many thanks for hospitality and medical attention."

"I hear General Trojan's voice." Colonel cried and his face turned pale. He looked around, confused and seemed did not know what to do.

"Yes it's his voice." Alex replied "Come and meet him Colonel." He then said good bye to rest of the audience and walked towards the exit.   Everyone, including servants followed him to see what was happening in the courtyard.   As soon as Alex stepped out they saw and heard General running up the stairs and saying; "Thank God that I see you safe your highness." He had stationed soldiers on both sides of the stony stairs as guard of honour and now running up the stairs he reached Alex and said, "I could not sleep last night." General went to embrace him while tears in eyes and said, "Allow me to embrace you, your highness; I am delighted to see you unharmed."

"Good morning General Trojan. Yes, I'm well thank you. But why did you bother to come yourself? Well, now that you are here I am sure you can thank Colonel and his family better, I have failed miserably." By then Colonel had dared to come closer, visibly shaky while his eyes were wide open and his face pale and covered by cold sweat. He saluted General Trojan with due respect and stood silent and confused. General responded his salute and said, "I will do my best your highness . Colonel Poxon, on behalf of his majesty the king I thank you and your family for sheltering our beloved Prince Alexander heir to throne. You will be rewarded generously." All present were shocked and Colonel seemed completely lost and speechless for a few seconds but as an army man managed to half control himself and while was shaking tried to say something and eventually did so.

"Prince Alexander?" cried Colonel "Oh my God, what have I done?" He kneeled in front of the assumed criminal who had miraculously transformed to prince, while repeating; "What have I done?" and began crying like a little child, "I was throwing you out. Please forgive me your highness."

"Please stand up sir," said the prince, "Man should not kneel in front of another man. Not even in front of my father, his majesty the king. Man should only kneel in front of God." He then helped him to rise and continued, "You have done nothing wrong to be ashamed of sir. I looked suspicious and you very rightly tried to protect your family. All that I will remember from last night is the kindness of your family and nothing else. You have wonderful children and you must be very proud of them." Colonel stood and straitened his back and looked at prince still tear in his eyes. General felt sorry for Colonel and said a few words in his ear to comfort him. Prince Alexander continued, "Colonel I must explain that I did not lie to you. I said my name is Alex Forman and that is true. I have lived with that adopted name for more than ten years. I wanted to live with people and be educated like ordinary young person. I have enjoyed these years tremendously but unfortunately with what happened yesterday it will no longer be possible. I said my father is General's servant that is also true. My father, His majesty the king has always said, "I am servant of the people." He is your servant, General's servant and servant of every person in this country. The rest of things you will read in papers later on to see all I said was true, I never lie, sir." He then called the butler and said, "Put that bag in the boot of second car and tell your driver to come and see me." He turned to Colonel again; shook his and said good bye. Colonel kissed his hand for which Prince Alexander seemed rather embarrassed and said to the General, "Let us go sir." He looked to the people standing in the cold at the entrance of the house and said "It is cold, please go in. Thank you all. Good bye." He then began walking down the stairs.

All the time fascinated audience were muted. They were all eyes and ears and it looked as if they did not feel bitterly cold weather of that unusual morning. Life is a magnificent play which is performed in a stage at least as big as our planet if not the whole universe and we are all actors and at the same time spectators in this play. It was interesting to look at this silent cast who resembled that reality but of course in a smaller scale even though; at that particular stage they were more spectators and had little share in acting except for showing their wonder and disbelief with their open mouth and staring eyes to add emotion and feeling to the drama. What this astounded and disbelieving audience had witnessed since the night before was not a common thing it was indeed incredible and unimaginable tale. No doubt that some of them could not believe their eyes or ears; thinking they were dreaming.

However Prince Alexander and General Trojan walked down the stairs. Colonel's driver unlike their first meeting presented himself with respect. Prince asked him, "Could you take us to waterfall? The answer was yes. "How long will take to get there?" The answer was half an hour if the road was cleared from heavy snow. He then gave some money to the driver too and thanked him for his help and said, "When I signalled, you start driving towards the waterfall. And tell that driver of truck behind your car, to follow you." Driver's answer was, yes your highness. "When we get to entrance of jungle you can return, don't come inside the jungle." Thereafter, his highness turned to General and said, "I feel sorry for your soldiers. Have they had breakfast?" General reassured prince that they have enough supply for the whole day. "Could you please order them to get into the trucks so that we could move? Those ladies and the child are still standing there. I fear they may catch cold." General gave necessary orders. Prince ordered the driver whom was holding door half open for him to get in the car and start the engine and said to General, "Please sir; get into the car first. I want to have one last look at these kind people and wave goodbye." General did so and Prince put his head on the top of half open door and for few seconds it appeared he was meditating. He then raised his head slowly, signalled to Colonel's driver to start driving, sent a kiss to his angel and waved to the others who were astonished observers of the extraordinary change of fate and circumstances.

When all the cars had left the courtyard, everyone retuned inside almost shivering. Enzel started jumping up and down while shouting, "I was right, I was right. He was a prince. I will tell my friends I got this present from a prince." Ravid looked at the back of watch and read, "To Prince Alexander on his twenty first birthday." It was signed by General Trojan. "This is too precious and very personal. I wonder if I could return to prince without offending him." Ravid asked his mother. By then Colonel had gone to library and locked the door. He wanted to be left alone for some time. Tophia had run to her bedroom to read the note. The last lines were; "Lady Tophia whenever you receive a letter which ends with these words and sealed as you see on this note, it is from me even if you hear I am no more:

They hanged me down the valley and left me to die there but God had another plan." She kissed the note and together with the beautiful ring put in a safe box and locked. She fell on her bed and cried; she did not know why? Back in the reception one of the old ladies said, "He looked like a prince anyway. I mean his manner, the way he talked and his generosity this morning all said he was prince."

"But last night you agreed with Colonel passionately that, he looked like criminals." said one of the guests, "No one said anything about him looking like prince except for that child." They continued arguing about who said what but Colonel's wife said nothing and went to the library to comfort her concerned husband. He opened the door for her and looked miserable. He was extremely worried what will happen to him for what he had said the night before and this morning.

"Nothing bad will happen. I assure you," said the wife, "Prince Alexander is loved by the whole nation for being a kind young man. No one has seen him for years of course, not even a picture of him but that is his reputation and now we know why. No one has heard anything bad about him. There were always rumours that he didn't like to live like a prince and wanted to be among ordinary people and that is one of the reasons why he is so much loved by nation unlike the younger prince whom every-one hates. He is very handsome, again unlike Prince Kohn."

"He was a student in the same university as our children" uttered the Colonel, "it is indeed unbelievable. He said he has lived with ordinary people for more than a decade. I'm ashamed of what I have said to him and I am worried what will happen. I am also ashamed of my silly reaction this morning. What the guests think of me now or our children?"

"I really don't think you did anything wrong this morning. I would have done exactly like you if I was in your shoes." She was trying to calm and reassure him using her background knowledge and skill as a nurse. "He is son of our beloved king and you showed your respect to that wonderful man and his son. I regret that I did not hug and kiss him when he said good bye to me. I won't have another chance like this."

"That would have been your precious present if you had done so. He is very generous."

"Yes it would be nice present. Cheer up man, everything will be alright. Mind you, I think he fancied Tophia. She has locked herself in her room with the ring and note he gave to her. I wonder if she has the same feeling as I. Now, let us join our guests. They are arguing about who said or thought that he looked like a prince." She then cuddled her husband and kissed him.

"Thank you my love. Yes, let us join our guests." Then they joined them in the reception room discussion about the event had not finished. Children were not there.

"We're still talking about the wonderful entertainment we have had at your mansion." said one the men, "We have seen the best play in the town free of charge with best meal and drink inclusive."

"Thank you cousin" said Colonel, "it was unexpected event. But I did wrong last night and humiliated myself this morning."

"Not at all my dear Colonel," answered his cousin affectionately, "not at all. Last night we were all suspicious of him and he really looked like member of a gang rather than student and this morning very rightly you paid appropriate respect to compensate our mistakes. Now, I do propose to celebrate this exceptional honour of having Prince Alexander as guest, here at this house. We had not seen him for more than ten years."

"Yes we must celebrate," said lady of the house, "very good proposal."

"We were planning to leave after the breakfast but after what happened we've decided to stay for lunch to talk and relive the event."

"By all means," said the lady, "but it will be late lunch."

"We do not mind at all to wait," said the cousin, "send for champagne and call the children to join us." They called the children. Enzel and Ravid joined them but Tophia refused to come. She was still on her room and by then had unlocked the safe box several times to read the note again and put that ring on her finger to acknowledge its outstanding beauty.   She was recalling every minute of the previous night and this morning. "He called me Lady Tophia," she said inside, "he kissed my hand; a prince kissed my hand."   Talking and laughter of the others were so laud that she could easily hear even though, there was some distance between her bedroom and reception room.   She could hear Enzel reminding them again and again that she was the only one to say he looked like a prince.   The guests, Colonel and his wife were really enjoying themselves and celebrating that unique occasion.   Enzel was busy playing with her precious present and Ravid was admiring that elegant watch, once again reading the inscription on it and wondering how he could return it to Prince Alexander without upsetting him.   In fact he was not entirely sure how he would face him or talk to him now that he knows who he is. "It is unbelievable," he said inside, "it is like a fairy tale.   A prince is living with the ordinary people, attending the ordinary school and university in preference to the royal life and luxury.   And not only that, he is a good basketball player too." He smiled at his last funny remark and tried to join the others and contribute to their conversation.

CHAPTER 5

On their way to jungle, prince narrated details of what had happened since he withdrew money from bank. General Trojan after listening for a few minutes could not control his curiosity and asked, "Why did you trust him?"

"Because someone, whom I trust with all my heart and soul; had sent hand written letter to introduce him."

"Who did?"

"General Trojan."

"Me? I have not sent you a letter."

"I know, listen to the rest of my ordeal." When the story reached to actual hanging scene he said something that he had omitted from his narration to Enzel. "Until then I had avoided revealing my true identity hoping that I could persuade them to get in touch with you, which I did not succeed, even after I had threatened them of your punishment. So when their boss was in the car and two men began to hang me I said who I was. One of the men said I believe him, there is rumour that Prince Alexander lives among the people. The other one said if we don't hang him boss will do himself. But I will teach him how to scape after we left; and he did."

Prince continued with the story and talked about the brutality of officer, in murdering both of his colleagues, how he managed to escape after that officer had left, how desperate he was to find a help and finally how he was picked up and saved by Colonel's children.

"I would have certainly died in freezing cold," he added, "had they not picked me up. Now sir, the reason I asked you to order the driver to ring the bell exactly at nine o'clock was to be able to organize myself and finish the expression of gratitude just before bell rings. I did not want to stay a minute longer after that."

"I can understand." said the general.   I also asked you to bring a team that could go down a deep valley. It was because of the two bodies there that I couldn't say over telephone. They either have ID to identify them or DNA will do so. And with that information police can trace the officer."

"Yes your highness.   You are a postgraduate student of law and are right about importance of that piece of evidence but did you not learn the name of officer?"

"You did not mention a name in your letter," said the prince jokingly, "and I'm afraid I did not bother to read his name on ID. I only saw it was from the intelligence office and the photo was his. Perhaps his ID card was also forged anyway."

"If he really was intelligence officer there aren't too many of them. We can ask for all the photos and you can recognise him."

"That is true; I will never forget his face." He answered and after a paus said, "Sir, there are facts that distress me more than anything else."

"What are they?"

"The fact that only few persons knew who Alex Forman was. The fact that no stranger was around when my father gave me the cheque and very few people knew that I was supposed to go to that party. "

"I see. Then, the conspirators must have informers within his majesty's household.   Very worrying if that is true." General said so and went into deep thoughts and appeared more worried than a minute ago.

They arrived to ground next to the waterfall; the crime stage. General asked the prince to stay in the car and went out to arrange the security. He feared there might be another attempt to assassinate the prince, possibly by shooting, if failure of their plan A was discovered by the conspirators.   Soldiers surrounded the area, having received their orders to prevent anyone entering there. He then brought army overcoat, hat and gloves to prince and having made sure all is well, he allowed him to get out of the car. The officer in charge of the investigations was introduced to his highness.   Prince described to officer what happened there the day before and showed where the bodies fell which were now covered by snow.   He also said, "We left some of what I was wearing yesterday in the boot of your car, just in case it was needed in the court and I am sure you will keep rope too for the same purpose.   Although I doubt you will find any useful forensic evidence in them, we have the main ones down there in the valley."

As they were all deliberating certain matters in relation to the event and were getting ready to send someone down the valley they heard noise and saw one of the soldiers bringing a middle aged man, with his dog following him. He had firmly held the hand of his captive behind his back.   He performed usual army salute to General and Prince and said, "Sir, this man says he has an envelope for you. He says a young man gave it to him few minutes ago."

"Please talk." General said to the man whom soldier had released his hands and passed the envelope to Trojan, Who gave it to you?"

"I don't know him sir.   Even if I knew I would not tell you because he begged me not to do so. I was walking with my dog when a young man ran after me.   He gave this envelope and said please ask one of the soldiers to give it to General Trojan, it is extremely important. Tell them that I don't want to get involved and I don't want their reward either."   General looked at the cover of envelope and read the words written on it: "Yesterday afternoon, I accidentally witnessed a terrible crime. I took these pictures and escaped from the scene when I saw that horrible man was killing the witnesses.   I have developed photos myself and I hope you will catch and punish him.   But I don't want to get involved; he is a very dangerous man. I don't want reward either. Don't try to find me and that will be my reward." General hastily opened the envelope and showed the photos to prince.

"That is him," cried the prince, "that is the murderer himself. Go and find the young man, we must thank and reward him."

"He has gone home sir," said the man "he asked me to wait until he has left the area before bringing the letter to you. He was scared. He came here hoping to see the police around. A lot of people walk in this area even in this season and the young man knew that, the crime would soon be discovered."   General gave some money to the man and let him go and said to prince,

"Your highness once we arrested the conspirators and the young man had no reason to fear we can advertise in papers and encourage him to come forward. But let us first concentrate on investigating the crime."

"You are absolutely right sir." The Prince answered and turned to the officer in charge and said, "Surely you would continue collecting the evidence but it appears we already know who the murderer is."   General gave certain orders, left half of the soldiers to help the investigating team and under the escort of the other half he and prince left the crime scene. Prince looked at all the photos again and said inside, "What a terrible day I had. I feel deeply sorry for those men and their families. They had to do what they were ordered but even in such condition they managed to help me to survive. I must find their families and help them as much as I can to ease their distress and grieve that they will naturally feel when they hear what happened to their loved ones. General was deep in thoughts and was watching the road very carefully; as he was still concerned about the possibility of another attempt to kill the prince. "Thank God" he said inside, "at least car is bullet proof."

CHAPTER 6

The main roads to city were not entirely cleared from the snow and ice yet, but the traffic was not so heavy. Therefore, General thought the head of intelligence department would not have any problem to get to his office while he and Alexander are on their way. Having said this to prince he called and asked the chief to do so.   Chief of the intelligence department lived in a village ten miles from the city. Then after few minutes of silence he suddenly said, "God was with you your highness. Not only he saved you yesterday but he also provided this crucial information to find out who was behind this crime."

"Yes you are right sir and that young man was the instrument in God's hand.   Now, if this man is really an intelligence officer we could find him in few hours' time before conspirators discover that I am not dead. They might even kill this man to leave no evidence or witness to their crime. Am I expecting too much or imagining too pessimistically?"

"Not at all, we certainly could."   General answered and began dialling the telephone "I will ask the head of intelligence to join us in my office." He did so and told him that he wants to talk to him about something serious in relation to the security matters.   He then said, "I am on my way to office and will meet you in less than an hour.   By the way, did you send one of your officers for a very secret mission? Yes that is the one I mean. Yes I asked you." He looked at prince and smiled while listening with interest, "So can you bring that letter with you? Thank you, that is splendid."   After finishing his call he turned to prince and said, "He says I asked him to send an officer for a secret mission. It is getting very interesting."

"Perhaps you did General." Said the prince and laughed for the first time.

"I am getting old; perhaps I did but forgot. We will soon find out. As you say if this man is intelligence officer his boss would recognise him when we showed the photo. The rest will be very easy, I hope." He then dialled again and this time ordered the security around his office to be tightened. He informed the officer in charge that the head of intelligence department is on his way to meet him. Then General said "Clearly I haven't told his majesty what happened to you. But as soon as we got somewhere in the investigation we must go together and inform him of this serious matter." Prince agreed and became silent. It was not snowing anymore and sun was shining but ice on the roads was constant reminder that, the weather is still very cold. Prince quite warm in army coat said inside, "I wished I had this with me yesterday."

As they were approaching the city, prince directed the driver through a road that, led to the address he wanted to deliver money. Once they got there he asked the driver to stop and got out of car. General who was terrified from what he saw; pulled him back and said, "No your highness, it is dangerous. Let the driver to deliver it."

"Don't worry sir," said the prince, "I have lived and played in these streets for many years, everyone knows me." He knocked the door and a man opened it and said, "Hello Alex. Nice to see you, come in."

"I would love to but I can't sir. They are waiting for me there," He pointed to the car and passed the envelopes, "This is from king, good bye." The man puzzled with what he heard; did not have time to say a word. When prince got into car; General had a sigh of relief. Prince became silent again and thought about his rescue the day before and about Tophia, "Probably, she will not believe but I will tell her one day." He was thinking about the university and his memories from more than four years of being there and studying. "So sad, I will not be able to finish the course." General left him with his thoughts and considered his next actions.

When they arrived to General Trojan's office, head of intelligence department was already there waiting for him. After the greetings and without introducing Prince Alexander General said, "Could I first see that letter please."

"Because it was top secret," said the chief, while giving the letter, "you sent it to my home address. That is why I had it with me at home." General looked at the letter it was genuine letter from his office. His face became red and he seemed lost in his thoughts. Since arriving to office two of his guards, the officer in charge of security and his secretary; had remained in the room. General asked them to wait outside and said to his secretary to stay in her office as she will be needed. Then after a minute or so he began talking while obviously surprised. "It has been typed by this typewriter on the desk, the paper is from the type which I use for top secret correspondence, it has also our reference number and a special code for that kind of letters, it bears my signature, it is sealed by my stomp and even has a PS with my handwriting but I have not sent this letter to you."

"When I received it sir," said the intelligence chief, "I checked all those points, which you just mentioned and made sure it is a genuine letter. I recognised your hand writing where you explain why it is posted to my home address. So I had no suspicion and so, didn't call you to confirm with you, particularly that you had asked me to send someone urgently."

"I am not blaming you. It is so genuine letter that I begin to think perhaps I've really sent it without realising; like sleep walking or something like that."

"Come on sir, confess that you did it," said the prince and giggled. "Cheer up General we will soon find out. Let us show the photo." General took one of the photos out of packet and showed to the man in charge, "is this the man you sent to see me?"

"Yes sir, he is Officer Hamis; the best agent that I have."

"Did he tell you what mission I sent him for?"

"No sir, you had strictly ordered him no one, including me,

should know about the mission and he is not a man to disobey the orders."

"Can we find him now?"

"Yes he must be at home. I can call and ask him to join us if you agree." General agreed and prince gave some suggestions regarding what to say over telephone.   The secretary found Officer Hamis and he was connected to his boss.

"Good morning Hamis. I am in General Trojan's office and we are talking about mission you have undertaken. Don't be alarmed but we think you might be in danger.   Please don't go out and wait for the officer I am sending to bring you here."   He gave registration number of car and continued. "Do not trust any other car and when the officer comes ask the code which is your birthday. All these precautions are to make sure that you get in right car with the person I am sending. Do you still have the letters which were given to you? That is good, please bring them with you."   They sent for him and General instructed the officer in charge of security to search him and make sure he is not armed before entering the room.

Half an hour later; Mr Hamis entered the room and said good morning to both General and his boss but when he saw the young man that he had hanged the day before is sitting there, he was shocked and became incredulous.   General showed him a seat next to his boss. He went forward, and while staring at prince, sat down and appeared doubting what he was beholding.

"Do you know this gentleman?" General asked. The answer was yes. "What is his name?" Alex Forman was the answer. "How do you know his name? Have you met him before?"

"Yes sir, I kidnapped and hanged him yesterday."

"Why did you that?"

"You ordered sir. I carried out the mission as you had instructed."   He produced the letter. General read it; it was a genuine letter without slightest fault in it. He then asked, "Have you met me before? Did I give this letter to you?"

"No sir, I came to this office and saw your deputy sitting were you are sitting now."

"You saw my deputy?"   General became very angry and seemed exceedingly concerned. He called his secretary to bring his deputy's photo.   He showed it to the officer and asked; "Is this, the man you saw?" No sir was the answer.   General brightened up with that answer and while sighing with relief said, "Thank God for that.   It would be devastating if it was my trusted deputy, but..." He did not finish his sentence and instead said, "Give me that letter with my handwriting."   The letter was produced and he looked at it with surprise, "It is my hand writing, I cannot believe it."   He then finished his previous sentence, "But you saw a General in this office. What was his name?"

"I didn't see his name but had two stars on his shoulder." Once again General called his secretary, "Recently all Generals had photo with his majesty. Please bring it here."   And once it was brought he asked the officer "Which one of these Generals was he?" He showed one of them. "No." General shouted, "Are you sure?" I'm sure sir, was the answer.

"He is my most trusted and loyal colleague. Are you sure officer. Look at the photo very carefully."   Officer looked and showed the same one. "Sir," he said, "I'm hundred percent sure it is him."

"He is General Leonard, it cannot be true. Explain your meeting with him."

"I called the number that is in the letter and made appointment, which I presumed was with you but, when I arrived I saw a different General who introduced himself as your deputy. He gave me your letter and repeated its content to make sure that, I appreciate the significance of the mission, which is eliminating an enemy. He also showed various top security documents to prove that, Mr Alex Forman has connection with foreign agents and is a grave threat to the national security and his majesty the king. He emphasised that no one except for him and you should know about the mission; not even my boss. He explained why it should be suicide not murder. He also gave me ten thousands dollar in cash for the expenses. I explained that there will be little expense for the preparation if any and I don't need that money to do the job. But he said once the mission was over I could either return the rest or keep as reward. Sir, I have not done it for money. I carried out exactly what was instructed in your letter and what I was ordered verbally as part of my duty to the country and king." The officer was going to say something else but at this point General cut him short and enquired, "Have you informed him of completion of your mission?" The answer was yes sir. He then asked his secretary to find General Leonard on telephone. She did so and General began talking as if he does not know anything.   "Hello Leon, how are you today? I am sorry to bother you at weekend which belongs to your family but I wonder if you could come to my office. I need to consult with you about an important matter before meeting his majesty." He listened and said, "Of course, you can come with me if you want. The road is not too bad but I don't want you to drive yourself if the driver is off. I will send my driver. I hear some noise, are you having your lunch? Isn't it early? No, I was too busy to look at my watch," he looked, "you are right it is nearly lunch time. Okay, don't worry I will have something to eat while waiting for you."   After that friendly conversation he called the officer in charge and ordered him to send a car with three guards to escort General Leonard respectfully but if he changed his mind and refused to come, to arrest him. "When he arrives search him," he added, "and make sure is not armed before entering the room."

"Now Mr Hamis, you were going to say something else when I interrupted you."

"I carried out instruction as ordered but I do not know what happened after I hanged him."

"Are you sorry that your victim has survived?"

"I would not say sorry but I am very surprised and disappointed of my failure sir."

"You will soon be very happy that you did not succeed. First, for your information neither of these letters are from me, they are fake. The hand written letter that you put in your victim's pocket is forgery too."

"I checked everything and I was certain that the letter was from you, sir." said officer "But I didn't check Mr Forman's hand writing because I did not have a sample of it."

"Well, they are fakes. Now, should I take it that you honestly did not know that you were hanging his highness Prince Alexander?"

"Prince Alexander? No sir, I swear."

"Well, he is the prince." General said so and turned to the chief of intelligence, "And you didn't know either I am sure. Only very few people were aware of the true identity of Alex Forman. I was just trying to see whether the conspirators had informed your agent or not."

"What a tragedy, my God. I feel partly responsible for it. I wished I had called you before sending this unfortunate man." All the time Officer Hamis had put his head down holding with his hands and sobbing quietly and muttering, "I ruined myself. I ruined my family." His boss began talking again, "Your highness, I do not know how to apologise. This betrayal and crime is beyond defence but I must say that Mr Hamis is the most loyal royalist and dedicated patriot. He would not have done what he did if he knew the truth. He is trained to obey orders without questioning."

"Please don't assume that you are in any way responsible for it." Prince began to talk after long silence he had held so far, "If General himself cannot find anything wrong with the letter how could you? As for this officer of yours, I can understand his situation. He is trained to obey without thinking. You call it blind obedience in army I believe. A normal human with normal state of mind cannot kill another human. You train them to do so; you train them to obey orders without questioning or even thinking. You order the soldiers to kill and they kill. Kill them you say; they are terrorists, they are enemy of your country, they are danger to your families and a threat to the national security and they kill. A few of them question you by saying; but sir, a lot of innocent civilians are killed too, question.

Don't worry you answer; they are sub-humans, not real ones like us. You brain wash them and they believe it and kill those so called sub humans in thousands and more. That is what they are trained for." Prince stopped the lecture and appeared very emotional. General Trojan kept the silence for a few seconds and then said; "Your highness is absolutely right of course. But I'm afraid in the army discipline and obeying orders is essential. Without that obedience you cannot defend the country or protect your nation at the times such as war or similar disasters. It is true of course; if the orders come from wicked leaders or commanders then regrettably blind obedience, would lead to many disgraceful crimes, atrocities and even genocides which we have seen in our life time and read in history books. Now, let me check you in that respect Mr Hamis. In this letter you are asked to destroy the letter. Why did you not obey the order?"

"I did sir," he replied tears in his eyes, "This is a copy. The instructions did not say that copying the letter is not allowed."

"I see the point. But I didn't notice it was a copy. Nowadays, advanced technology amazes me. Sometimes copy looks better than the original. However, after hanging your victim you also killed two other men. Does the order mentions eliminating anyone else apart from Alex Forman?"

"Yes sir."

"Where does it say?

"You have ordered no one except for yourself and your deputy should know about it. The only way I could fulfil this part of the instruction was to kill them. That is what I understood from your letter."

"What about Mr Forman's friend?" As general continued to finish his question, the officer looked at the face of alarmed prince who suddenly had leaned forward to hear the answer and in his mind went back to his act after the hanging.

On the way out of jungle, the intelligence officer decided to fulfil his orders and make sure no one knows what was done. He went straight to the house of prince's friend and as he had not learned his name asked the man who opened the door, "Please could I see Alex's friend?"   Once he appeared the officer said, "Hello, it is me again. Alex sent me to ask you a favour for him."

"With pleasure; what he wants me to do?" asked the student.

"I think it's something about his college. He will not be able to come on Monday. I have written what he said. I am not used with that kind of terminologies. But sir, I'm very tired and thirsty.   Could we go to this pub, opposite to your house please?" The student did not mind and when they sat in a corner the officer said "I'll buy you a drink, what would you like?" He preferred beer. So, the officer bought two glasses of beer and paid for it. While the girl was busy to bring back the change, he dropped poison in student's glass and joined him.

"Let us drink to Alex's health." He said and drank more than half of it to encourage young lad to do the same. "Alex is a very good lad and seems from a very rich family too." Officer said.

"Not really, but General Trojan knows his father and supports him."

"I see. Then let us drink to General's health." He drank and she student did the same.

"I will tell you what Alex wants but I must go to bathroom first. I'll back in a minute." But he did not return. He watched from a distance and when he noticed poor student is dozing went out of pub. He knew the effect of poison is almost instant. All this went through his mind in seconds and then he heard the rest of the question.

"He saw you in the bank. Did you kill him too?" He could see the prince was waiting for his answer but didn't want or did not dare to distress him in that place and time so he replied; "That was different. He didn't see me hanging his friend. I was pretty sure that he would recognise prince's hand written letter and would be convinced that he took his own life."   He saw the prince was relieved to hear his answer and leaned back. General said, "I don't think Leonard will be here for another half an hour or perhaps more.   We better eat and drink something." No one wanted to eat therefore he ordered tea, coffee and fruit juice. Later on he politely asked the prince if he wanted to use his private bathroom in his huge and magnificent office which he did.   He also ordered one of the guards to escort both chief of intelligence and his agent to the bathroom in waiting room if they needed. "But they are not allowed to talk to soldiers." Some of the guards were already stationed there.

Once all were refreshed they waited for General Leonard in silence. Each one of them was engaged in his own thoughts. Officer Hamis regretfully was thinking about his practical role in the conspiracy that, he had undertaken without having slightest suspicion about the reasons behind the mission.   He sincerely believed that he was doing a service to country and king and had no idea about the true identity of Alex Forman.   "I wished Alex had told me who he was." he said inside and then immediately questioned himself, "Would I have believed him?" and answered, "No let us be honest, I wouldn't." It was too late anyway and he feared for the grave consequences and fate of his young family.

Head of intelligence was sorry; for not confirming the request with General before sending Hamish and was blaming himself, why he did not ask later on whether he was happy with the agent he sent. General himself was thinking about the possibility of informers in King's palace as well as his own office and at the same time, was extremely concerned that Leonard the officer whom he had trusted so much' was involved in that terrible crime.Prince was mainly thinking about his father and Tophia, not much about his ordeals at that moment of the time.

CHAPTER 7

For those who were in General Trojan's office it appeared a
long and frustrating wait even though it was only forty five
minutes from the time he had talked to General Leonard, or
Leon, as he called him over the telephone. They were busy
with their thoughts and silence had been kept for some time
when suddenly noise from outside startled and alerted them
all. Leon had finally arrived and was fiercely objecting for
being searched. The door was opened by chief officer and the
expected General stormed in with red face and seemed angry.
He reluctantly saluted and said, "This treatment is unacceptable and very insulting." But, when he saw that the agent whom
he had sent for the secret mission and the young man, he had
presumed dead, were in the room too he knew that he was in
serious trouble. The colour of his flushed face changed from red
to purple and then completely to white with no trace of life on
it. "You betrayed me." He said to the officer.

"No, he performed the mission precisely as you had ordered."
Prince intervened, "It is my fault that I did not die, I apologise."
General Trojan had neither risen up from his seat nor had answered his salute and at this point he showed him a seat next
to the officer. Leonard sat and remained silent. General asked
him, "I see that you recognised the assassin and surely you know
Prince Alexander too. But this gentle man is head of intelligence department in case you haven't met him before." Leonard
said nothing. General showed the first letter and asked, "Did
you send this letter to the department of intelligence?" Yes was
the answer. "Did you give this letter to this man beside you?"
Yes was the answer. "Did you also give this handwritten note

from me and this hand written letter from prince to him?" Yes, he answered. "How did you manage to produce such letters that neither I nor prince can find any fault in them?"

"One night; I brought someone with me who can open any door and safe." Leonard began talking after all of his one word answers. "I bribed the guard and cleaner to keep their mouths shut. He opened the door of corridor leading to your office, then this door and that safe in the corner. I typed those letters on special papers which you keep in the safe and used reference number and code, proper for such letters and sealed them with your stamp. The signatures, PS note and hand written letters are done by a clever artist who can copy any writing or signature instantly, by just seeing once."   "It is amazing and clever job I have to admit." said the General, "Allow me to recap what I have learned so far. Like a burglar you broke into my office, prepared those letters and in my name asked head of intelligence department, to send an agent to my office for a secret mission.   The agent called the number that you had given in the letter and you made an appointment to meet me in my office.   But once again you broke into my office, met him here and introduced yourself as my deputy. You instructed him to kidnap and hang Alex Forman knowing that he was Prince Alexander. But why did you that?"

"I had my order from someone high that I did not dare to refuse or disobey him."

"There are few people above your status in this country. Who was him, me?

"No sir." said the honourable Leonard who was now turned to a miserable criminal.

"Who was he then?" insisted General to hear.   But suddenly the guilty man shouted on top of his voice with anger and sadness, "Look General, I've been too coward to resist a bully, an intimidation and too greedy to refuse a lucrative offer.   I have betrayed his majesty the king, I have betrayed you and I must immediately be court marshalled and executed.   But before I die give me a chance to save the king.   Call him and tell not to take any new medicine from his physician. Part of this plot is to poison the king. For God's sake don't waste the time and do it right now before asking any more questions." There was a thunderstorm in the room. Both Prince Alexander and General Trojan rose to their feet without realizing why they did it and sat again. Prince looked extremely worried but General Trojan soon managed to control himself and as if he is in war, began commanding. "Find his majesty in his palace immediately and," he said to his secretary, "connect him to the phone number one."   He turned to prince and said "You talk to your father on that phone." He then rang the emergency bell and said to his chief of staff, who had jumped inside hastily, "Find the officer in charge of security in king's palace and ask him to call me on this number immediately." He showed the second phone on the desk. The secretary had not found king yet, when the officer in charge of the security of palace called him, he said, "This is General Trojan. Increase the security to critical level. No one is allowed to enter or leave the palace. That applies to the members of royal family. Where is king now? Did you say he is having his lunch? Okay, he must remain there. No one should enter or leave that room. We are trying to find his majesty on the phone to request him to remain there until Prince Alexander and I come there. Do it now and call me if any problem or news." He was sweating and seemed very concerned. Rest of the people in the room, including guards who had entered room following the emergency call, were shocked.   Prince impatiently was watching the phone. After agonising few minutes of wait finally he was connected to king. "Good afternoon your majesty, it is Alexander. I beg you don't take any new medicine if physician has given any. I know sir; I had to say it first, before any explanation. I hope you have not taken any new medicine." he listened "I am happy to hear it. There was a plot to poison you." After saying last sentence he chocked, tear filled his eyes and could not talk anymore. General took the telephone and talked to king himself, "Good afternoon your majesty. Please do not worry. Prince Alexander is absolutely fine; he just got a bit emotional. We will come and explain everything to you. But at this stage, we beg you not to take any new medicine or anything suspicious and please do not leave the room yet. We've increased the security to critical level. No one is allowed to enter to your room until Prince and I arrive. We will finish our investigation shortly and meet you in an hour's time." He listened and replied, "At this stage I can only say that there was a plot to kidnap the prince and poison you." He didn't mention hanging and listened again, "Your majesty we do not yet know the reasons behind this plot or who has planned and ordered it. No your majesty, he is not harmed; he is fine. I pass the telephone to him." He did so and prince who had now recovered said "Sorry father I was just very worried about you, I am okay now. Yes, I can talk to mother." he waited, "Hello mum, yes I am fine. We are investigating something at the moment but I will come to see you soon. Good bye for now."

Having calmed down General Trojan faced to Leonard and said, "Thank God that you have not totally killed your conscious and loyalty and warned us to prevent a catastrophe, or I hope we have done so. Now tell us who persuaded you to do this, which I know is so uncharacteristic of you?"

"I cannot tell in front of these people sir." General asked the guards to take chief and his agent to waiting room and said, "Stay there with them. They are not allowed to see or talk to anyone." He then asked chief of staff to stay out "Close the door and make sure no one comes in." and faced to Leonard, "Okay we are alone now. Who did it?"

"It was Prince Kohn."

"No, you are lying." Prince said angrily.

"I am sorry, that was him. I can prove."

"Explain yourself." General ordered.

"Few weeks ago prince invited me to his palace and said, he had a grand design to become king and make me head of the army in your place. He wanted me to prepare a letter in your name and ask the chief of intelligence department to introduce a reliable agent for a top secret mission. He also suggested that instruction to intelligence officer should be in your name too. He said he could easily ask one of his men to kill Alexander any time he wants but that would lead to investigation which he did not want. You have already learned details of the plot and I am not going to repeat.   However, he gave me one million dollars in cash and said more will come after he becomes king. He said his majesty's physician has already agreed to poison the king. He also said once in power, he will retire you sir and make me head of the army."

"Did he not want to kill me?"

"No that would have led to investigation too. He threatened me that if I did not corporate; his men will gang rape my wife and children in front of my eyes. Not only that, he will also accuse me for plotting against the king and has influential people; to support such accusation. As I have already confessed sir, I was coward enough to fear such a threat and greedy enough to accept such offer. I don't want to face my family again; I'm too ashamed.   Please order the execution immediately."

"You will be executed," said General coolly, "but before that; you must explain everything to his majesty."   He then summoned his chief of the security and said "Send an officer and few guards to Prince Kohn's palace to inform him that, his majesty wants his attendance in an urgent meeting to discuss an important matter.   They should escort him to king's palace but if he refused to go they should arrest him." The officer in charge was very surprised and looked at Prince Alexander who seemed very sad and drawn in his thoughts. "Do it immediately, I'll call his palace and let the body guards know." He then asked secretary to find the security officer in Prince Kohn's palace and gave necessary instructions to him once connected.   During all these activities the man in front of the desk and the prince sitting next to the General were in their own worlds and virtually unaware of the commander-in-chief's efforts. Equally, General not aware of their state of minds was busy with preparation for meeting with king. "Call his majesty's physician," he said to the secretary, "and tell him to go to palace as soon as possible. Let him know that I want him to be present in an important meeting with king." He called palace and asked the officer in charge of security "I'm going to call his majesty and inform him that, I've asked you to escort him to his office and Queen to her apartment. Once you have safely done it wait for us in the gate, there will be two cars. The people in the second car are also allowed to enter. I have also asked King's physician to come and Prince Kohn will come with an escort." He then asked his secretary to find the king on phone again and when he became available on phone he said "Your majesty we have now finished the enquiry and are coming to report it. There will be Prince Alexander and other people with me to tell the full story.   I have just asked the officer in charge of security to escort your majesty to your office and I suggest Queen should be escorted to her apartment if you agree. Details of plot will be painful to her." He listened and said, "Thank you for agreeing your majesty." Energetic General called the chief of staff again and said, "We will be going to king's palace shortly. My car and another one should be ready immediately.   Discharge all the extra staff, officers and guards and keep only the ones that are needed. You can lower the security level." He then called his secretary and said "You can go home, thanks for your help."

Once general was informed that, the cars are ready, he jokingly said to two dreaming persons in the room, "Wake up now, we are going home. I mean we are going to meet his majesty the king." They came out of their worlds and began to prepare themselves to accompany him.   General sent someone to let chief of the intelligence and his agent to come back to office. He turned to chief and said, "Thank you very much for your help and your time.   We are going to repot the plot to king and I really don't think you need to come. Please go to your family, they must be worried now."

"It would be an honour for me to meet his majesty," said the chief, "It is also possible that, he might wish to ask questions in relation to our unfortunate involvement in the conspiracy.   If you allow, I would like to come too." General agreed. This is the code of the safe in my office sir." Leonard began to talk "Please send someone to bring the red box that I have kept there. I'll inform the security that I am sending your man. He could bring it to you in the palace while we are with his majesty." This was arranged too.

When they reached the gate of King's palace the officer in charge of security came to meet them. General told him that Prince Kohn as well as king's physician have been asked to come too and they should be brought to his majesty's office. He also instructed the officer to reduce the security to bellow critical level as details of plot has been revealed now. "It does not seem there is immediate danger to his majesty's life." General Trojan concluded, "But things might change, so be alert." Gate was opened and two cars entered. The officer drove his car in front until the entrance of the palace in order to open the door for them as he knew the guard will not allow anyone to enter, even General Trojan.

CHAPTER 8

King's workplace was an imperial mixture of private library, conference hall and of course an office. In that particular day, king had ordered his armchair to be placed beside the desk rather than sitting on the chair behind the desk which normally would do. He had now threw himself on that comfortable armchair but, seemed restless and unhappy with his anxious wait. There was another chair beside him for Prince Alexander. Soon the arrival of General Trojan and companions was announced. They all entered and showed due respect to the king. Prince rushed to his father kissed his hand and was hugged and kissed by his majesty. The rest of the arrivals and two guards remained standing until king asked them to be seated. General briefly said something to the guards and then began his report. "Your Majesty, I am deeply sorry and concerned that our report to you will be very distressing. I've asked Prince Kohn and your physician to attend too and we have to wait for their arrival to explain details of the plot. But briefly, the plot was to kidnap and hang Prince Alexander and poison your majesty." King startled and looked at prince with alarm and noticed the lacerations on his neck. My God," he said mournfully, "did they hang you?" At this point arrival of physician and Prince Kohn was announced and they entered the room. Prince bowed and kissed his father's hand but as there was no other chair beside king he looked around with dismay. General showed him a chair at the end of row beside physician and he sat there with angry look. General Trojan was sitting close to Prince Alexander, next to him was Leonard then Officer Hamis and chief of the intelligence department and thereafter physician and Prince

Kohn.

Having gained king's permission General Trojan began talking "Your majesty at this stage of the report I ask Leonard to explain what he did rather than why he did it. Leonard told his story exactly as he had said to General and prince; earlier. And while he was explaining what and how he did; General showed king the letters; step by step as the narration went on.

"That is unbelievable." said the king, "I have always considered you as one of the most faithful officers in the army. This is shameful betrayal of your king, your country and a crime beyond my imagination. Why did you do this?"

"He is a traitor and he himself must be hanged immediately." Prince Kohn said with anger. Trojan looked at him with surprise and said to king, "Your majesty, allow intelligence officer to explain what he did and why. If you permit, Leonard would answer your majesty's question after we have reported distressing part of this disgraceful conspiracy. I am afraid it will upset you but it is necessary." King allowed and the officer explained his involvement exactly as he had said to General and Prince Alexander. Once again he decided not to say anything about the killing of prince's friend. King was clearly distressed when he heard it all and looked at his son's neck once more and said, "Thank God you are alive. What a terrifying situation you were trapped in. How did you escape?" Prince had not said a single word since he shouted at Leonard in Trojan's office by saying "No, you are lying." Now in presence of his father and knowing details of plot he felt too emotional to describe his ordeal again. So he looked at General Trojan imploringly and signalled to him to narrate on his behalf all that he knew. He began by saying "Your majesty clearly his highness Prince Alexander is too distressed to talk about that horrifying experience but, he has already explained to me what happened after that officer killed two of his colleagues and drove away." He then explained how one of the men facilitated his subsequent escape, how he manged to pull himself up that rope and run all the way to find a help and how he was rescued by the Colonel's children whom took Alex Forman to their house where he spent the night without them knowing who really he was. He did not say anything about the Colonel's suspicion and his attempt to throw him out. Prince was pleased that General omitted that part and showed his appreciation by nodding his head and smiling. "My dear brother" said Prince Kohn, "what a terrifying experience you had. I can't wait to punish these criminals." Once again Trojan looked at him with surprise and for a second he thought perhaps Leonard had lied to him.

"Can we now hear why you did it sir?" King said rather impatiently.

"Your son Prince Kohn asked me to do this, your majesty."

"What?" Cried Prince Kohn and got up to punch Leonard's face but he was immediately stopped by the guard whom already had their instruction from Trojan, "I asked you to hang my dear brother; the brother that I love as much as my parents? Did I plot to poison his majesty my father whom I will give my life to defend him? Who would believe this nonsense? Take that traitor out and execute him."

"Your majesty," General intervened, "please allow Leonard to explain why he makes such an accusation." King accepted his request and Leonard repeated all he had said to prince and General, earlier that afternoon. When he finished the story Prince Kohn laughed loudly and said, "I don't know why we are allowing him to lie so insolently and live. Father, this is a plot by my enemies against me. I've made many enemies; they now want to discredit me and take their revenge."

"Do you have any prove to your accusation against my son?"

"Yes your majesty. Your Physician can testify."

"Did Kohn ask you to poison me doctor?"

"Please forgive me your majesty." The physician pleaded.

"Have you given poison to me?"

"I was threatened by....," said the physician but he could not finish the sentence and after a pause continued, "I can't say. I am scared. No, I have not given yet." He then began crying.

"But you were going to give it. Who told you to do this?"

King shouted angrily. Physician began stammering clearly unable to say a word and appeared extremely agitated. Prince Kohn intervened and said, "Your majesty please spare this old man form saying a lie. It is clear that he has been threatened to give false evidence." He then began comforting the physician by saying, "Don't be afraid. No one will hurt you. I know what they are up to and will explain to king." He then turned to king and said, "Father it seems conspiracy is much bigger than I thought. It is more likely that republicans are behind this plot. They meant to remove my dear brother out of their way then, poison you and put all the blames on me to make me unfit to be a king in the eyes of nation. Once power vacuum was created they could achieve their purpose. Is there anyone in this room not to see it? In such an outcome they would take the opportunity and declare the end of Monarchy and birth of the Republic."

"That is a possibility." King agreed and appeared rather relieved that his son is not behind such a disgraceful crime. Even Prince Alexander and General Trojan thought for a minute that perhaps Leonard had not told the truth. Prince Kohn seemed triumphant for a minute and they all looked at the accuser for the explanation.

"I wished it was true your majesty but I am afraid it is not." he declared, "I have a reliable witness to confirm that your own son made me to be a traitor at this age for which I should have been executed by now and will be shortly. But first you should hear the truth."

"You can bring hundreds of witnesses, I am certain," Prince Kohn said sarcastically, "but I won't accept any one as witness except for my parents, my brother or perhaps General Trojan although I am not sure he is not behind the plot himself. He is very popular and could surely be the first president of the republic."

"You have confessed enough crime to be executed shortly" king said, "but your claim that my son is behind the conspiracy is unbelievable. For God's sake could you tell the whole truth before you die?"

"Yes your majesty I can. After I accepted Prince Kohn's proposal with all my greediness and fear, I began doubting its reality. I was also ashamed of myself to fear a boy and his gang where I had never feared in the battle fields. Conspiracy seemed too big to believe so easily. I thought perhaps prince wants to see how loyal I am. Or he wants to take revenge and put me in trouble because he knew that I had criticised his way of life. Therefore I requested another appointment and once more met him in his palace. After greetings and some introductions I asked; your highness do you really wish me to kidnap and hang your brother? He said yes." Here Prince Kohn interrupted him and said "What a dirty liar. Are we going to let this insane to insult me further?" Trojan and Prince Alexander had not heard that part so they were keen to hear more from Leonard. King ordered him to carry on without any more interruptions and Leonard continued. "I said why don't you simply ask one of your associates to kill him in university? He answered, no that will lead to investigation and I do not want it. I said; I am not so sure that the physician would poison king. And I fear that you might be left with the grief of losing a brother without achieving your goal. Don't worry about the doctor, he said; I offered him something that he could not refuse. I said what about General Trojan he might not agree to retire. Prince replied; you can be sure that he will retire. I will be strong king with absolute authority not like my weak father whom has given up most of his power to the parliament, judges and this Generals. When I say retire, he will retire. If I say die, he will die. Finally I asked his permission to suggest a small change in his plan? He allowed me and I said; please ask the physician to delay poisoning the king until Alexander's body is found. And then when your father grieves and seems unwell, doctor can gradually give the king the poison pretending that new medicine is a tranquiliser. In this way king's health slowly deteriorates and dies without any suspicion. He said; that is an excellent idea. You will be a wise head of the army."

"I kept quiet because his majesty had ordered. But I have never seen a liar as shameless as you." Prince Kohn said, "Do you reallythink anyone would believe these disgusting accusations?"

"Yes your highness they will. I have a reliable witness." At this point Leonard asked Trojan to open the box. He did so and passed him a small cassette player.

"Who is this reliable witness of yours?" Prince asked mockingly.

"You are my witness, your highness."

"Really; why should I confirm your dirty lies?" But he had hardly finished his sentence when the conversation that Leonard was referring to; began being broadcasted. Intimidated traitor had secretly recorded his last conversation with prince.

"Stop it, you bastard." Shouted Kohn and hurried to take the tape player out of Leonard's hand but once again was restrained by the guard. "Please ask him to stop it," but tape continued. "Stop it." he repeated and fell on his knees while both hands were held behind him by the guard.

"Please forgive me father." he pleaded and began weeping loud.

Tears silently poured down from the king's eyes. Cassette player continued revealing the conversation precisely as Leonard had reported. Prince Alexander looked at the king with utmost sorrow, kissed his hand which was resting on arm support of chair and put his head on father's hand and quietly cried. It was a mournful scene of a very sad play which no one had seen before. No one had ever beheld the king crying. All the eyes were wet and a dead silence pursued after the tape finished broadcasting the confession. No one dared to break the silence until king himself began talking. "As a father I am a failure. I have brought up a son like you Kohn. I am responsible for the crimes you and your gang have committed. Your sins are my failure. I must talk to my people and ask their forgiveness for my failing in responsibilities as a father. They have every right not to forgive me.I ignored and covered up some of your mischiefs; foolishly hoping that you will grow up and embrace the righteousness." Prince Kohn was still on his knees and crying silently. King signalled to the guards to seat him on the chair and free his hands. General Trojan dared to say "But your majesty; you have also brought up a son like Prince Alexander whom the whole nation adores."

"He was brought up by the people not me." Replied the king and once again silence filled the room. A minute or so later, he first dried his own eyes then raised Alexander's head, kissed him and tenderly dried his eyes too. Gloomy silence sustained while everyone was deep in his thoughts struggling to comprehend the extra ordinary event of that day. Once again Trojan broke the dead silence and said, "Your majesty I can court- martial Leonard and execute him. I can also ask judges to decide about the punishment of Officer Hamis and your physician. But you have the absolute authority to decide about their punishment without involving the courts. Please advise me what I should do with them."

At this point Prince Kohn stopped crying but continued keeping head down anxiously and fearfully waited for his father's judgment. After some delay king said "Leonard should talk in radio and television and tell the nation everything that he told us except for participation of physician. This tape should be played for the people too." Here, Prince Kohn started weeping again but his father ignored him and continued "Money must be returned to treasury. Retire him with full entitlement as if he had reached the retirement age and put his family under our protection. And only then try him in court-marshal and do what the verdict was delivered that I assume will be execution by the fire squad." King paused for few seconds and said "Retire this officer with full entitlement and put his family under your protection. He should return the money to treasury and be tried in appropriate court. If the verdict of the judges was execution by hanging then, contact the families of those murdered men to enquire whether they are prepared to forgive him. If they forgave him, reduce the punishment to imprisonment. As for the physician dismiss him from our service and send him to a town of his choice to continue his private practice." Everyone was anxious to hear his majesty's judgment regarding his son.

"What about your brother?" King asked Alexander, "How should he be punished?"

"Oh brother, even after hearing your own words, captured in the tape, I still find it difficult to believe that you were behind this shameful conspiracy. If you had just told me how desperately you wish to be king; I would have taken myself out of your way. I would have requested his majesty to make you heir to throne. I can forgive you for plotting to kill me but I will never forgive you for what you had planned to do with our father. You must be punished for that."

His majesty turned to Trojan and said, "No trial for Kohn. Put him in prison immediately but separate from the other prisoners. He should have all the necessary facilities for a relatively comfortable life in prison and food as he wishes. But he must not have access to alcohol, drug or women. He should have no visitor except for those who have to attend his needs. Send a team of trusted guards to make sure that our instructions are followed." Prince Kohn fell on his knees again and begged for the forgiveness but, his father suddenly stood up and said to Alexander, "We will now go and see the Queen. She became extremely distressed after hearing that you were kidnapped and I do not know how she can tolerate this appalling news." He then turned to General Trojan and added, "As usual I leave the difficult part to you even though I see you had hardly any rest. God help all of us." And he left the room without saying anything else and refused the escort. This was very unusual behaviour of the king, which clearly reflected the extent of his distress. In important meetings he would usually dismiss everyone except for prime minister and Trojan for further discussion to add finishing touches to the conclusion of meeting or the decision made. However, in this particular meeting, when one of the officers brought the red box, Trojan asked him to remain in the room.

And as the king was declaring his judgments and recommenda-
tions; he kept writing notes and passing to that officer in order
to prepare for the implementation of orders. He had hardly had
slept or eaten since the night before, when prince called him
from Colonel's house.   By the time King left the room most of
the staff or officials that he had summoned, had arrived or were
on their way. So he began the hard part, which king had referred
to.

CHAPTER 9

It was late in the afternoon of that memorable day and by then; authorities of prison, radio, television and all the extra guards and officers had arrived to the king's office which was now a headquarter for General Trojan. They all waited patiently to receive their orders.   He first talked to Prince Kohn privately. "If someone else had done what you have done, without any doubt would have been convicted to death by hanging. Now put your head down and let the guards to take you to the prison. As soon as possible I will request from his majesty to agree a different punishment for you outside the prison." Once prince was taken to prison, General talked to heads of the radio and television and informed them of king's order.   Leonard, while attended by the guards; was taken to the studios for recording a surprising show for that night and the following days. Physician was ordered to get ready for leaving the capital and was allowed to go home.   The intelligence officer was sent to jail and once all the others had left the room, General said to chief of intelligence, "Once again I thank you for your help sir. You must be tired, I am exhausted myself. Let me take you home."

That evening (and the following days); the whole nation heard and saw, the most thrilling and unimaginable drama. People exhibited different reactions to the news.   On one hand they were appalled to learn that, their adored prince was kidnapped and hanged and his majesty the king was supposed to be poisoned.   But on the other hand they were happy to hear that the prince escaped and conspiracy was exposed. They were glad that Prince Kohn is in prison and were over the moon to find out that, rumours turned out to be correct and beloved prince had indeed lived among them for years.   The extent of jubilation was beyond any description amongst individuals and families who had actually met their prince and lived with him either as one of their friends or a friend of their children.   And of course, the euphoria amongst the Colonel's children was exceptional indeed.

Prince Kohn remained in the prison and all members of his gang were arrested. Those who had committed serious crimes received long imprisonments or executed. Some were sent to the rehabilitation centres hoping to transform them to good citizens. King's dismissed physician moved to another town to start his private practice. General Leonard was executed by the fire squad after implementation of his majesty's recommendation. Officer Hamis received death penalty. Families of victims were contacted but they did not agree to forgive. They argued that his excuse that he had followed the strict order was not acceptable at all . "He could carry out his mission differently," they said "either by doing it alone or trusting his colleagues that they would keep the secret. Also, murdering the student was an unforgivable crime and beyond defence by any logic or excuse." So, Hamis was hanged.   Appropriate arrangements were done for the families of two men who were murdered by Hamish; as far as the retirement and pension was concerned as well as the compensation for the loss of their loved ones.

When Prince Alexander heard that his innocent friend was also murdered by the officer, he was devastated and immensely grieved. He locked himself in his room and lamented for days and hardly ate or slept adequately. No one could persuade him to stop mourning and join the family or friends.   Eventually the king had to go to his room himself in order to console his son and instruct him to meet his friend's parents to express his condolences and find out what help could be offered to them.

Prince went to see his friend's parents.   Over the years of his friendship with him he had been in their house numerous times and they had always treated him like a son.   Now he was a prince who had come to visit them not Alex Forman a friend of their son. They had the same love towards him but were uncomfortable and felt too inferior. But prince behaved with them as he had always done. He expressed his condolences and said how devastated he was when he heard the sad new. "I really feel responsible for this tragedy." He said tear in his eyes, "When he suggested coming inside the bank, I should not have accepted. He was murdered because he saw the officer who kidnaped me and that criminal didn't want to leave any witness alive." These words were uttered with his melancholy appearance and a broken voice, so parents of his friend lovingly consoled him and thanked him for coming to see them. Prince asked what he could do for them but they did not need help. "I know that your son's desire was to support his siblings' higher education when he starts working as a lawyer. I beg you allow me to fulfil his ambition." With tears in their eyes they agreed. Later on, prince opened bank accounts for all of the siblings and deposited more than enough money in each account; for their higher education. But they could only have access to their money when they were eighteen years old. He also contacted their solicitor and instructed him to pay the rest of their mortgage and return the deed of house to family. Of course, nothing could have return their beloved son to them but genuine grief of Prince Alexander, who had lost a good friend and his unconditional love and sympathy that he had expressed for that family; was appreciated by parents and consoled them a great deal.

*

Alexander was not enjoying the life as a prince and, was bitterly longing for good old days when he was living amongst ordinary people. He went in disguise to see his friends or invited them to his palace to enjoy their company. This was the palace that belonged to both brothers but he hardly had lived there. He sent a couple of letters to thank Tophia, enquiring if there was anything he could do for the family. A few times he went to the university in disguise and watched Tophia from a distance without her noticing him. He also visited his brother in the prison and appointed consolers and psychiatrists, to help him in his rehabilitation and send appropriate books for him to read. Of course for all these supports he had gained his father's permission.   The king had noticed Alexander's boredom and had attributed it to the fact that he was missing his friends and company of the ordinary people but he had hoped that, his son would soon get used to a different kind of life in royal family.

One afternoon when Tophia in the university garden was walking with few girls to join her brother and return home, a middle aged man approached her. He presented a small note to her and said, "Miss Tophia, may I have a word with you please?" She took and looked at the note and began trembling. She asked her friends to go without him and if they saw her brother to let him know that she will be few minutes late. They did not want to leave her alone and after a few steps stopped and turned back. She waved to them and said, "Go, don't worry about me. I know this gentleman very well."   She did not of course but the note was enough to trust him. They reluctantly left her but kept turning back and looking at her again. The sentence that she had read many times and familiar seal; was on the note. The man told her, "Please go and sit beside that gentleman on the bench; he is waiting for you.   You know who he is but please do not address him with his title.   Don't worry at all, I will be watching from this side of the road and there are two body-guards hiding just behind him."   While still shaking she went and sat beside the gentleman and said, "Good afternoon sir."

"Hello lady Tophia, how are you?"

"I am fine thank you."

"Are you concerned that your boyfriend might see you?"

"I don't have boyfriend." Interestingly as she was saying so, a young man approached rather hastily and asked Tophia if she was okay and she said, "Yes I am. Please go and let my brother know that I will be a bit late."   After he went away disguised Prince Alexander said;

"He sounded like a boyfriend." Tophia laughed and replied, "He is my cousin and father has asked him to protect me I suppose. I'm sure the girls informed him. I don't know why every-one wants to protect me."

"It is because you are too beautiful."   Tophia blushed and kept quiet but prince continued; "I don't want to take your time more than is necessary. However, I want to tell you that I had seen you before. Of course, I didn't immediately remember that night of course. You too may remember; one day in canteen you accidentally spilled your hot soup on my trousers and jacket."

"Oh, yes I remember. I was very sorry and ashamed of myself but you did not get angry."

"How could I have time to get angry?   I was captivated with your beauty. Later I enquired and found out that you were a Col-onel's daughter. So I tried to forget all about you. I was just a ser-vant's son, a poor student and felt that I did not have a chance." Tophia said nothing and kept shaking and sweating. Prince also kept quiet for a minute but suddenly said, "I love you.   Would you accept to be my wife?" Tophia was shocked to hear such a proposal from a prince and began to cry. "I didn't ask you to cry. I asked will you accept to be my wife. But perhaps my disguised face frightened you."   Shaky Tophia tried to control herself and managed to say "If you asked this question, from any girl in the world; every single one of them would say yes.   Because of whom you are and what your real face is behind this disguise; no one could resist such a proposal.   Now if I say yes, there is no value in it. It would be similar to yes from millions of girls in the world. I wished you had asked me this question when you were a poor student.   So my answer is no sir, I cannot."

"Even if you are right about all girls in the world that I do not think you are; the difference here is that I don't love them, but I love you."

"No sir, you should marry a princess or someone equal to your position."

"I don't agree with you but let us go; I see your brother is coming and appears worried." They got up and began walking towards Ravid, and when they reached him he asked, "Are you alright Tophia?" Prince replied, "Yes she is, doctor."   Ravid startled and shouted, "I've heard that voice is your high..." but his sister put her hand on his mouth and said "Hush" and pushed him towards the car which was parked nearby. "Good bye sir it was nice to see you." She said hurriedly.

"You didn't see me, you heard." answered the prince and laughed, "But yes; good bye."

The man who had talked to Tophia was following them watchfully and, as soon as siblings were in their car he too led the prince to his car and bodyguards got in the second one behind it.

"Your highness" asked the man while driving, "what was the result of your meeting, if I'm allowed to ask?"

"Atta can you stop calling me your highness?"

"No your highness I can't, you are a prince."

"You called me Alex almost all my life, why not now?"

"You were servant's son then but you are now king's son. But I could compromise. I will call you Alex when we are alone but your highness when others are present too."

"Okay, that is a deal."

"So what was the result?"   Prince recited all the conversation and ended up by saying, "she said no to my proposal."

"That no means yes Alex; believe me. She is just scared of being king's daughter in law. Leave it for a while." This man was the most trusted person in prince's life.   He had been with prince since he was a little child.   Throughout the prince's life amongst the people he was the guardian, advisor, provider of his personal needs, a trusted link between him and royal family, in charge of his financial affairs and responsible for all the security arrangements without prince's knowledge.   This constant care and protection had lasted for nearly twenty years. He truly loved Prince Alexander like his own children.   Atta was a happily married man and had three young children. King and Trojan trusted him too and valued his outstanding services to the royal family.

Alexander decided to send letters to Tophia from time to time and leave their next meeting and his proposal for another time. He accepted Atta's interpretation and felt that Tophia too is in love with him. "My parents will love her I am sure." he said inside, "She does not need to scare but if she wants; I can live like an ordinary person again and practice the law, when I am qualified. By the way I must do something about my final exams." And he remembered his friend, "So sad, he is not with me anymore. We were going to practice together." Tears filled his eyes. Atta noticed and said, "Alex, I know whom you are thinking of. It was very sad but you must accept that there are tragedies in life that we cannot prevent. We must live with them. He was a very good lad. God bless his soul." Prince remained in his own world until they reached his palace where he was not enjoying the life or at least not as much as he did when he lived in university camp or in the rented students' flats.

Sometime later Alexander discussed his future plans with king and queen and made it clear that, if his brother was genuinely rehabilitated and transformed to a better man; he would like to pass the honourable role of heir to throne to him. He would like to live amongst the people, marry with the girl he loves and work as a lawyer now that he is fully qualified for the job. He also informed his parents; who was the girl that he loved to marry with even though Tophia hadn't yet accepted his proposal. The king was very sad to see how reluctant his favourite son is to succeed him and was not optimistic about the Kohn's transformation to a person whom would be readily accepted by the nation as a king. He was also concerned about the safety of Alexander and his future family, if he once again lived as an ordinary person. King believed that living among people would always make him a target for the enemy and difficult to protect him and his children all the time. But he loved Alexander very much and did not want to push him to a situation that will make him miserable.

"Why don't you marry her now? We could decide about where you should live, later. Let us make your mother and the people happy with a grand wedding party."

"She does not want to marry a prince."

"Nonsense, invite Colonel's family for dinner; I will talk to the girl. What is her name?"

"Tophia; but please allow me to think about it."

There were no further discussions about his plan for a few months and the prince remained hopeful that, soon his brother will prove their father wrong by his success both in rehabilitation and higher education.   Later on, he privately consulted Atta and explained to him what he wished to do in near future or as soon as is pretty sure that Kohn progressing in right direction.   Atta warned him that his hopes about the brother are unrealistic and impractical and added; "Even if there were positive signs of changes in imprisoned prince, most likely, it will be short lived and in any case people will never accept him as king."   Alexander remained optimistic and asked Atta to help him in implementation of his plan.

He had now passed his final exams and was allowed to practice as lawyer but obviously in reality this was not possible. "How can I practice while I am heir to throne?" He said inside, "How can I marry Tophia if she doesn't want royal life?   It all depends on my brother's efforts and sincerity in rehabilitation. Of course; if I succeeded in my plan."

CHAPTER 10

It was now almost eight months since Prince Kohn had been kept in a solitary confinement and Alexander had tried very hard to help him.   During this time he visited him many times and provided everything that he could think of or was recommended by professionals; to help his brother in his rehabilitation.   He was hoping that he will change and become a good person worthy of being king. Indeed there were some definite signs of progress and Kohn genuinely was ashamed; not only because of conspiracy to kill his brother and father but also, because of all the wickedness and crimes he or his gang had committed.   Being totally deprived from the hedonistic life was not so easy to tolerate to begin with. But the more he became conscious of the magnitude and ugliness of his crimes and offenses; the more he felt regretful and ashamed of himself. This awareness and acceptance of guilt, made it easier to tolerate the life without the pleasures which he was addicted to. He realised that at very young age he was unfortunate to mix with the wrong sort of people and learn the wickedness from those villains, rather than pursuing the advanced education like his brother.   Alexander encouraged him to continue his education while in prison and promised to provide everything which he needed including best tutors.

In spite of the General Trojan's interventions and repeated appeals to king, his majesty did not agree to send him aboard or keep at house arrest. His majesty said, he must remain in prison until is really changed to a better man. In fact the king was blaming himself for the double standard in punishing those who were involved in conspiracy. He knew that anyone else in son's place would have been hanged. He was also uncomfortable about his decision; treating him so differently in prison. But the fact that Alexander forgave his brother consoled the king as a reason behind lighter punishment and he also convinced himself that, separating him from the other prisoners were just for the security reason. This subconscious self-defence somehow comforted him but not quite. However, perhaps these thoughts were behind his reluctance to accept General's requests.

One day, Prince Alexander went to visit his brother and after congratulating him for visible progress he had attained, and genuinely encouraging him to carry on with the good work said; "My dear brother you are a good man by nature and it was merely bad luck or perhaps even our fault; not to have looked after you properly that you met those criminals and rascals and fell in their trap.   You have now fully reformed yourself and trying to catch up with your interrupted advanced education. You now deserve all the respects that people have denied ou from it which of course you'll admit; it wasn't their fault."   At this point Prince Kohn wept and said, "When you are so kind to me I feel even more ashamed of myself. I know that I don't deserve respect from people. With what I have done and with what people have heard about me; I am sure that they will never forgive me. Like our father who does not forgive me, and I confess that he is right in not doing so and I don't blame him. How could I blame anyone, after what I did?"

"They will all forgive you once they see how much you have changed. In fact his majesty has agreed that you should be transferred to your palace. You'll live there as before but of course with some restrictions. I am taking myself out of your way and one day you will be king."

"What do you mean?"

"I have some plans. You will soon hear that I am no more. Was it not what you wanted?

"Sorry brother but I have to say; don't be so ridiculous.   And please for God's sake do not remind me of my crime anymore. I thank God all days and nights that I did not succeed."   He really seemed regretful of his past and it was obvious that he had changed both physically and mentally. Alexander felt sorry for his brother whom had lost weight and appeared depressed.

"Okay I will not." answered Alexander after a pause, "But please promise me that you will continue with your rehabilitation as well as education. And please promise that when you are a king; you will serve the people like our father."

"I won't be a king but I promise to do all I can to change and educate myself. You frighten me; the way you talk suggests that you are not coming to see me for some time."

"That might be true. I have done all I could, you don't need me anymore."

"Please don't say that." They continued talking for an hour or so and when Alexander was saying goodbye he repeated his appeal; "Please don't forget your promise about the education and becoming even a better man than you already are. So long my dear brother."

Few weeks later, royal family and the whole nation heard of the most disastrous accident. Prince Alexander's car had fallen into the river at the bottom of a valley. The door at driver's side was open but there was no trace of prince. He had been seen driving fast before the accident and no one else was in the car. This shattering news devastated the people and royal family. In Colonel's house Tophia fainted when she heard the news and after being revived run to her room while crying nonstop and locked herself there. Kohn in prison was stunned and said to himself, "My God he was serious. My brother is no more? I cannot believe it."

After that unhappy news, prince's faithful protector Atta immediately rushed to see the king and Queen. The meeting was strictly private and at the end of it king summoned the chief of staff and ordered him to broadcast in radio and television that while the search is continued to find Prince Alexander's body, there should not be any national bereavement. People should be consoled by explaining different possibilities. For example it is possible that following the crash and head injury; prince has temporary loss of memory and currently staying somewhere to recover. Or perhaps he is wounded and certain people are looking after him without knowing who he is. It is also possible that, he escaped injury but suddenly decided to take advantage of this tragic accident and once again live amongst the people, disguised. This is very likely because we know that he has been longing for it since the day he had to return to royal family after being kidnapped and hanged. Of course the possibility that body was washed away to the sea could not be ruled out and, the king would appreciate prayers from all people who loved the prince.

Immediately after the meeting with king, Atta went to meet Tophia and handed her a letter and said, "Please read it in your room and, for God's sake don't show any reaction in public." Tophia hurried to her room, opened the envelope and as soon as she saw the coded sentence and familiar seal, began crying with joy as those signs indicated that Alexander was alive. She had remembered him saying "Whenever you receive a letter which ends with these words and sealed as you see on this note, it is from me even if you hear I am no more." The letter in fact confirmed that prince was alive in which; he had asked her to keep the secret only for herself. He had also requested her not to display any change in her emotions after receiving this letter and continue with what she had expressed following the news of accident. He had informed her that he was on his way to live in another country in Europe. "Wait for the next letter," prince had concluded, "and trust Atta as much as you trust your parents and siblings." She kissed the letter and put it in the box alongside the other tokens she had from prince.

In the meantime police authority formally announced that the search to find prince's body has failed and their conclusion is that, river has swept away and carried the body into the sea. King sent message to the nation that he would like to remain hopeful to hear from his son and continues to pray for his safety. He asked people to pray for him and not give up the hope. Few weeks later Atta returned to Tophia and reported, "Now that

Alexander once again is a servant's son and lives with ordinary people, prince wants to know whether you would accept his love." Tophia smiled and then cried. "I can take that smile as a yes," continued Atta, "but what is that cry for and what does it mean?"

"It means definitely yes, where is Alex?"

"Do you have passport?"

"Yes."

"He asks me to take you where he lives so that you could get married."

"Oh Mr Atta, how can I do such a thing without my parents' approval? Not that they will not approve it; of course they will but prince has asked me not to tell anyone."

"Yes there is a problem there. We have to tell them and trust that they will not disclose our secret to anyone."

"They won't, I am sure. You tell them please." So he went to meet Colonel, his wife and Ravid. When Atta informed Colonel that the subject is top secret and a child should not hear it. He sent Enzel to her sister while the meeting was going on. Once Atta informed them of the safety of prince and his intention, they were over the moon. Colonel and wife's jubilation was both because dear prince was alive and also because he had proposed to marry their daughter. Mother cried with joy and Ravid was delighted to hear the news and of course he already was aware that his sister and prince were in love. Colonel assured Atta that they will protect the confidentiality of prince being alive and living abroad and they will facilitate their daughter's journey. Trusted man Atta informed them that based on the prince's instructions he would accompany Tophia and be witness to their marriage. "No one else is planned to attend in the simple ceremony," said he, "and there will be no party either." Mother was very upset that there will be no wedding party and she will not be present in such a happy occasion. But, she understood the reasons behind it.

Once Tophia joined Prince Alexander they married in a civil registration office with his real surname inserted on the marriage document although, he had begun living abroad and had just started PhD course in international law, with adopted name of Alex Forman which was on the certificates from Maxim University, brought by Atta. He continued his higher education in international law and they both enjoyed a relatively simple life. Tophia kept herself busy with art and responsibilities of wife and was very happy indeed.   Prince Alexander, now Alex Forman did not get in touch with his friends for security reasons although he very much liked to do so. However, both sides of the families were in regular contact secretly.

CHAPTER 11

Prince Kohn was released from prison and returned to his palace but he was not allowed to be as free as before in his day to day conducts. Queen visited him occasionally but the king neither visited his son nor allowed him to come and see him. Prince Kohn was puzzled with what could have happened to his brother and could not get any more information from people around him; certainly nothing more than what he had already heard while in prison. He knew of course that on the order of his father as long as Alexander's body had not been found there should be no grieving. "But why so much mystery around it?" he kept asking himself.

To begin with, he continued with his advanced education and frequently saw consolers and psychologists; in order to make further progress in rehabilitation but this did not lost for long. Former associates who had escaped the punishment or were sent to the rehabilitation centres; managed to get in touch with the prince and came to see him in his palace regularly. Such reestablishment of contacts and influence they had on him changed everything. Few months later he was back to his hedonistic life, even worse than what it was before his imprisonment. The advanced education and all the efforts in becoming a good person were forgotten. His life now comprised of gambling, alcohol, drugs and women whom were smuggled into his palace and nothing else mattered to him. Reports kept arriving at king's desk and made him both sorry and very angry. One year after his release king had no choice but to send Prince Kohn back to prison with the same arrangements as before.

But the news from Alexander's front, which were brought by

trusted Atta exclusively to the king, queen and Tophia's parents were happy and pleasant ones As a matter of fact if it was not for the earnest request and wish of the prince and king's promise; they would have let the nation be aware of the reality and rejoice.   Truly in that case; there would be enthusiastic national celebrations. Not only because of being comforted that he is alive but also because of hearing that their beloved prince was married to one of their own daughters in the city and not to a princess in another realm or daughter of another ruler. But Alexander had convinced his father the king that he would be by far much happier if he was left alone to live a normal life with ordinary people and definitely, he did not want to be king after his father had returned to God.   He wanted the people to give up hope of his return and at the same time accept that Prince Kohn truthfully is a changed man and worthy of succeeding their beloved king. Whenever Atta visited Alexander and Tophia, he brought them all the news from home as well as gradual decline in Prince Kohn's efforts to be a good person. Alexander was also informed that king is not as healthy and as active as he used to be. Obviously this news made him very sad and concerned about his father's condition as well as the future of country. This made him to think seriously about his duties as a son and as heir to throne. He appreciated the fact that; if the king is not as fit and as healthy as he used to enjoy and, is getting too old to carry heavy burden of responsibilities on his shoulder alone; he would naturally expect help from a son whom he trusts.   He began to question himself; "Is it really my generosity to deny myself of becoming a king and pass that chance to my brother or is it my excessive selfishness to prefer my own happiness and ambitions to the duty to my father and country?" He remembered the people's love to him as well as father's love and hopes. He appreciated the nation's and the king's expectations. So, he realised that he could no longer ignore his responsibilities and no longer he should only think about his own wishes and the priorities in his private life, although he was truly very happy living with Tophia and they were expecting their first child.

However in spite of all the concealment; the Queen and Tophia's mother secretly travelled abroad to meet the couple and in one of these occasions, receive another good news first hand that Tophia was expecting first child and ultra sound had shown it was most likely a boy. His majesty did not travel to see the son and daughter in law.   He was in mixed emotional state and not so good in general health. On one hand he was immensely disappointed and indeed ashamed of having a son like Prince Kohn and on the other hand was proud of Alexander except that he couldn't understand why the heir to throne so much disliked his royal status and, unwilling to succeed him as a king. On one hand his majesty was delighted to see his favourite son is married to a beautiful lady, from whom he had only seen photographs and there is a grandson on the way but on the other hand was depressed not to have the opportunity to give a wedding party worthy of a prince. "People would have loved it." He said to himself.

Health of king was deteriorating fast and reports from the prison about Kohn were very disappointing. These realities made everyone in royal family and Government, quite concerned and understandably uncertain about the future. The best doctors in the country and some of the best from other nations had been invited to examine, investigate and treat this ailing monarch, but prognosis seemed rather gloomy. Therefore a meeting was convened involving the senior officials from the Cabinet, Parliament, Judiciary, Intelligence and Military service to discuss various aspects of the problem. In spite of his illness king chaired this strictly secret meeting himself.

"I fear that I will not be able to execute my duties" said the king "unless these doctors find miraculous solution to my poor health.   I am so ashamed to admit that; our son in prison is a disgrace and we cannot count on him. Our only hope Prince Alexander who is indeed pride of our family and the nation is in self-imposed exile."   All the officials present in the meeting were shocked to hear that prince was still alive. The secret had been kept so successfully that even the prime minster or head of intelligence services did not know anything about it. The only person who already knew and did not show any reaction was General Trojan. "Yes, we kept it secret from all of you and the people." King continued "It was Alexander's earnest wish to live abroad as an ordinary man and very much hoped that, his brother will be transformed to a better person and formally replace him as heir to throne. He genuinely does not wish to be king and wants to serve people as a lawyer. I have promised not to force him to succeed me if Kohn continued his rehabilitation successfully. Alexander assumed that if Kohn hears that he is no more he will work harder to change and be accepted by people. He was sure that, that will be the case. He was planning to come back home as soon as I formally introduced Kohn as heir to throne. I am really amazed by Alexander's generosity and his power of forgiveness; it is beyond my understanding. Kohn conspired to hang him but he forgave his guilty brother and did all he could to help him to change and become a better person. He did it by providing the best tutors, consolers and psychologists for him. He sent him all the relevant and useful books and encouraged him to pursue advanced education. It seemed to us that he had made some progress but we were wrong. Perhaps I should not have released Kohn from prison so early; I blame myself." King stopped talking and appeared sad and generally unwell.

The meeting lasted for more than an hour while king still present and all aspects of current state of the affairs were discussed and considered carefully. The conclusion was that Kohn is not a choice even if had succeeded in changing to a better person. "People would not accept him" said General Trojan, "and unrest could follow." It was decided that, the burden on king's shoulder will be reduced but his majesty would kindly continue with his duties as long he can until Alexander could be persuaded to return home and help his father. In the interim, it was agreed that General Trojan would deputise the king; wherever he couldn't attend or whenever he didn't feel well to execute his duties as a king. Very soon the whole nation knew that their beloved prince was alive. How did the people find out was a puzzle for the king. The meeting and whatever was discussed in it was supposed to be secret. But his majesty the king did not try to find out who spread the joyful news. "Joy of this nation is more important." King said inside, "I hope that we will all behold him soon, it is more than two years since I last saw my son. I've seen some photos of course. What a beautiful daughter in law and grandson I have. God bless them. I hope that I will see them before I die."

CHAPTER 12

Four years had passed since the infamous conspiracy to hang Prince Alexander and poison the king.   The criminal prince was still in the prison and people's prince was now a father and still living abroad.   Prince Kohn somehow had got hold of the drugs and was an addict by then; behaving very badly in prison. Looking after him had become a nightmare for the guards and authorities of the prison.   His health was not satisfactory either, mainly from excessive use of alcohol and drug. The criminal gangs in prison would somehow get all these things to him, no matter how hard the guards tried to stop them.

Prince Alexander on the other hand was a happy father and had attained the PhD degree in international law.   Although he was enjoying a happy family life but, he was extremely concerned about the sad news from home land.   Since everyone became aware that prince was alive and living abroad he managed to visit his ill father a few times; all arranged secretly and quietly by his trusted man Atta.   Having accepted Atta's earlier verdict, he had now given up the idea of changing his younger brother to a better man and preparing him to be king. That acceptance was of course with utmost regret but unfortunately prince Kohn had practically proved it that his older brother's ambitious plan was unachievable.   Alexander decided to return home and help the king but hoped and prayed earnestly that father will live for years and he will not be crowned as king yet.

While prince was in the process of preparing to return home, totally unexpected and sad news shattered him. His brother had died in prison. In spite of what Kohn had done to him, in spite of the immoral life style that he had chosen for himself at such a young age, and in spite of all the crimes he had committed against the innocent and defenceless people; he still loved him.   He truly had wished to help him to change and one day become a king. He had no ambition himself to succeed his father.   Now the circumstances had changed; his brother had died and father was seriously ill. The cause of Kohn's death was announced as over dose with drugs but police did not make it clear whether it was accidental or he committed suicide. And if he had really committed suicide was it because he was so ashamed of his past crimes and present condition or was it because he had heard that his brother is alive and returning home to help the dying father and effectively become a king? Whatever the answer the news was sad for the family.   Both king and queen naturally grieved for losing their son even though they were not proud of him.   "I feel responsible for everything he did," said the king, "even in some way responsible for his final act."   King went on air and in spite of his extreme weakness and obvious poor health talked to the nation while lying in bed.   It was distressing for the people to see him so wasted even before hearing how seriously ill their king is.

"You have heard the sad news that our son Kohn died in the prison. No matter what he did in his short life that as a father I am both ashamed of and feel responsible for; nevertheless he was our son and no one would blame parents' bereavement in such tragedies. Sometime ago I asked you to forgive me for my failures as father. I now humbly ask you to forgive his crimes and mischiefs too and I pray that God will forgive and bless his soul. He had his punishment in this world." King seemed very sad and unable to carry on but after a minute he continued, "The other news you've heard is that I am terminally ill and have very little left to live. Sadly I cannot serve you as much as I wish. I hope that I was a faithful servant to you all and you will pray for me." King rested for some time before being able to carry on with speech, "However, I am delighted to say that I also have good news for you. You already know that Prince Alexander is alive and since that car accident has been living abroad. During his residence abroad he continued his education like any other student. He has now PhD degree in international law. I suppose we can call him Doctor Alexander." King smiled for the first time since he was on air, "He must be the first prince in the history to have such a degree but I may be wrong. That is not important; the important thing is that he is coming home." He became emotional and tears fell from his eyes. After another pause he said, "He loves you and you love him as your own son, I know. Indeed you have brought him up and that is why he is such a good person. He is retuning tomorrow; welcome your beloved prince, welcome your king. I have no doubt that he will be able to serve you much better than I tried to do. He will always remain grateful to you all for having him amongst you for so many years during his childhood and early years of adulthood. During his life time he will be regarded as the greatest and the best king in the world and later in the history. Yes he will be remembered so. Welcome our king tomorrow. I will feel honoured to be his subject before I die." This was a live broadcast and when king could not go on any longer it was cut off prematurely, and later on announced that it was exhaustion and his majesty felt better after the rest.

The nation remained in front of the radios and televisions with mixed feelings. Sorrowed to see and hear that the king so wasted and ill and rejoiced to learn that, their prince is coming back home. The latter feeling gave them energy and much hope and they began preparations for receiving the future king in their arms and pressing him to their hearts.

CHAPTER 13

Prince Alexander returned home with Tophia and their son. Hundreds of thousands of the jubilant people went out to welcome them. They filled both sides of the route from airport to king's palace. They were carrying numerous placards displaying on them; welcome home Prince Alexander, welcome king Alexander or even we love you Doctor Alexander, and were shouting all these and more. Prince and his wife waved from inside the strictly protected vehicle with tears in their eyes. They were driven straight to the palace and as soon as they arrived; Alexander, followed by Tophia and son on her arm, rushed to the king's room, where he had lain on bed very frail but, eagerly was waiting to see his son again together with daughter in law and his grandson whom he had not seen before. It was an emotional scene where both joy and grief had mixed. King, queen and indeed all who were present in that room were happy for the return of Alexander and his young family but at the same time sorrow and anxiety had filled the room because king was clearly very weak and fading. Prince and Tophia kissed king's hand and his majesty kissed them both as well as his grandson. Then with a very low voice said to the future king, "What a beautiful queen you will have." and looking at his wife affectionately added, "Like your mother, like my beautiful queen." After a pause he said to queen, "I want to be alone with Alexander." Queen led everyone out and closed the door behind her. He talked to his son for a few minutes but was too weak to continue and fell sleep or fainted from exhaustion and joy of seeing him.

The king's physical weakness was increasing quickly and it

was obvious that, he will soon die but, he wished to have the opportunity of addressing the nation one more time, in spite of his fragility and lack of energy.   His wish could not be ignored and so this was immediately arranged and the cameramen set their equipment around his bed.   He began talking while his son was standing beside the bed and queen together with Tophia and her son, were sitting just behind the king's bed.It was the most unusual broadcasting and the whole world could see it happening.

"I am dying and wish to say good bye to you before my last breath and once again ask you to forgive me for my shortcomings." He paused for a minute "Please pray for me." There was another long pause. "I wish to see Alexander as our king and have the honour of being his subject before I close my eyes for the last time."   He paused again and tears fell from his and prince's eyes. "I formally abdicate at this minute so that he could be crowned tomorrow. This will provide me the honour of dying as one of his subjects not king." King could not continue and seemed to have passed out.   Physician was called. He examined and announced that king has merely fainted from the exhaustion and should not be disturbed any more.

The following day Prince Alexander was crowned solemnly but with simple ceremony. He was brought to his father's presence as soon as the crowning completed; so that he could fulfil his wish and see his son a king.   Tophia and son came too as well as the queen. King opened his eyes and when he saw King Alexander, smiled. He raised his finger as if showing him to all present and said "My king." Then he signed to Tophia to bring his grandson closer to him. She did so and the dying monarch gently touched the boy's head, kissed him and Tophia and said, "Take him away I do not want him to see me dying."   Tophia and boy left the room. He then turned to King Alexander and with some difficulty managed to utter "Your majesty, please allow me to kiss your hand and die as a faithful subject."

"No father." Alexander cried. He hastily took the crown off his head, bent down, got hold of his father's hand and kissed it while weeping.King reached to his son's eyes as if trying to prevent him crying and touched his face while smiling faintly. He then closed his eyes and minutes later stopped breathing. The trace of a faint smile was still visible on his lifeless face.   The queen, now queen mother who was quietly weeping all the while; embraced her son with all her love to him and they both cried loudly. The officials including the prime minister and General Trojan who had accompanied their new king after he was crowned and were waiting outside rushed in to pay their final respect to the old king who was laid on the bed in ultimate peace.   They expressed their condolences to King Alexander and queen mother and comforted them.   Then preparation for the funeral was immediately begun under the leadership of prime minister.   And the death of a great king was announced to the whole world.   Alexander, who was greatly sorrowed for the loss of his father, began feeling the burden of responsibilities as king but he had already a grand plan in his mind. He was determined to execute the plan as soon as the time for national mourning was over.

Grand state funeral of deceased monarch was attended by virtually all the kings, presidents and various heads of states in the world and more than a million grieving people followed the coffin. All the attendants in funeral whether heads of the states or ordinary people paid their respects and expressed their condolences to the young king and queen mother.   Young king was very much touched by kindness of people to him and the extent of their love to his father.   All the governmental departments, offices, schools, universities and the shops were closed for three days and the national mourning continued for one week.   Throughout the grieving period mass prayers were conducted in all religious centres.   Although the old king had done nothing immoral to ask for forgiveness but nevertheless, he had repeatedly asked this from his people.   The only thing that people could think of was in relation to Kohn that king had thought partly responsible for his crimes and failing to control him but they had forgiven him long time ago.

Once the official mourning period was over, and the guests had returned to their countries, it was announced that King Alexander would speak to the nation via radio and television. He briefly discussed his plan with the prime minister and General Trojan and made it clear that it was for their information not approval. For years Alexander had thought about the fair system of governing the people and had come to conclusion that there is no system without weakness or defect but certainly some are better the others. Perhaps that was one of the reasons behind his reluctance to succeed his father. But the circumstances had forced him to be king and now he wanted to find a way around the problem of flaws in the systems. Of course, he was aware that his father had already done a great deal in making the system more just and fair and truly he had served the people rather than merely ruling on them. The old king had converted an underdeveloped country to one of the best in that part of the world and had laid foundation of democracy for that nation. Alexander appreciated father's achievements and service to people but he thought more fundamental changes are necessary. He was seriously concerned that the existing constitution could be misused in future and once again lead to dictatorship. History was a witness to his concerns and he knew only hundred years ago, his grandfather succeeded a dictator and began the reforms," which was continued by his father. "This constitution," he had said many times in debates, "can lead to another dictatorship in future." So, he took the first step by delivering his what it would be remembered a historical public speech.

CHAPTER 14

In his formal speech; he first thanked the officials of the government and all the people for their kindness and condolences to him and queen mother.   He thanked for all of their prayers and expressed his belief that his father's soul is blessed by God, not only because of his virtue and justice in life but also because of those prayers.   "I am sure that," he said, "my father in heaven is happy that the nation had remembered his humble service." Having fully conveyed his gratitude he turned to main purpose of speech, "I was hoping that my father would live for many more years and no one would need to think about the successor but regrettably the most advanced medicine lost the long battle with his incurable illness. Truly, I was hoping that patience, time and labour of the counsellors, psychologists and the best teachers in country; would change my unfortunate and mislead brother to a decent person, a righteous man and to an honourable son worthy of succeeding a great father but he proved that his transgressions are irreversible.   Now I am afraid you are left with me; a lawyer by education and intended profession. Thank God that, I am privileged to be surrounded by the most capable and virtuous men and women, whom were chosen by Great king. So I don't need to change anything at least for the time being. In other words business as usual, as far as the running of country is concerned.   All of the professionals, officials and authorities in various departments will remain in their posts and will continue serving the people.   Parliament will run its term and army will be led by same commander in chief whom king transferred his power to.   Today I want to discuss about the system of governing the country.   I know there are people in our country who think the system of republic is more democratic and they have good reasons to say so.   In the monarchy you have a king with ultimate power in his hand.   He has inherited this from father, you have not chosen him. If he turned out to be a bad person, a tyrant and an oppressor; then you have a huge problem in your hands.   We may not always be so lucky to have a king like my father who saw himself a servant to people rather than an emperor, who appointed a good person as prime minister and asked him to select a cabinet from amongst righteous individuals. A king who founded the nucleus of democracy in this land by setting up the parliament and advising you to elect members for that parliament in order to protect your interests, express your visions in the debates and on your behalf; vote on the legislations that are presented by the government.   My father did all these reforms and even relegated his position, as the commander in chief, to one of the best soldiers in army.   But we will not always be as lucky as we have been over recent decades. I loved my brother in spite of all the wrongs he committed and I understand that it is not right to talk about someone who is no longer with us to defend himself and clarify his conducts but, to appreciate what I am trying to say, just visualize for a minute; what kind of king he would have been if he had succeeded in murdering his brother and father? What sort of the people from his notorious gang would have run the country and for how long?   He was very young, so sad.   I feel guilty that I as an older brother did not look after him and I couldn't prevent him from mixing with bad people in the first place." Here, he paused briefly to supress the emotion that had temporarily distracted him from the main direction of his speech and then continued, "But in the system of republic, you choose your own man or woman to be president and form a cabinet to run the country.   By no means do I say that there could be no flaw in such system, far from it. A clever populist could manipulate and excite imagination of the people by saying what they want to hear. He could talk the way people talk; to attract them.   He could include in his manifesto, the matters which people are interested at and, by the power of propaganda etc. could persuade them to vote for him in order to win the election. Once elected to begin with he could afford to use the same language that they comprehend and repeat the same pleasing slogans with which he won the election in order to ensure continued support of same excited mob. But once by using crowd's support he managed to consolidate and fortify his position; disregards all of the promises he made in manifesto and becomes an autocrat to pursue his own plan and protect his own interests. We have read some examples of it in history books and you know that even today we have some of these so called elected presidents who have remained in post for as long as they live, either by changing the rules of election or the constitution. However, in my opinion there is no perfect system to govern and run the affairs of a nation with justice. But surely some systems are more democratic and fairer than the others.   I don't even believe freedom and democracy are without problems and defect of their own.   We can debate all these in more depth and details later on but at present my intention is to ask, what system you wish to have in this country? Do you want the monarchy or republic? I have asked the prime minister to arrange a referendum for this purpose as soon as possible.   All parties, groups and anyone for that matter; whether right or left, whether royalist or republican should have equal opportunities for campaigning and debating their views and philosophies and, all should have equal access to the media.   They should have equal finance from the government for their campaign and spreading of their views.   Referendum must be observed by the independent international observers. I ask you to listen carefully to the debates from all sides, think wisely about the reasons they put forward in supporting their ideas and make fully informed decision before you vote. Please use your brain not your heart when you vote. Put the emotion aside and think about your children and future generations too. Transition is not so easy of course; if you vote for republic. So, to save time a group of experts have already been commissioned to prepare draft of constitution for the republic, to be debated in parliament; after the result of referendum if republic was your choice. I will talk to you again once the result was known. God bless you all."

People were astonished of what they heard. Here they had a new king, their own beloved prince who had just been crowned to succeed his departed father and the first thing he does is asking them to decide whether they want him to remain the king within the existing system of monarchy or, give it up to an elected a president in the new system with a new constitution. It was totally unexpected move from king which surprised the whole world. Referendum was the subject of debates and dialogues in every corner of the country after the speech and before even government set a date for it. Reaction to king's speech, discussion and debate amongst his former classmates was in particular very interesting and hot. "Good old Alex, he has not changed at all." They said, "Neither living abroad nor having PhD changed him, nor suddenly becoming a king." They talked about him; how dignified and confident he was and how they had assumed him son of a servant whom was sponsored by a General and indeed how they all had loved him as a polite and down to earth student who intellectually was well above anyone in the college. They remembered him studying and scrutinising different ruling systems in the world, different religions and ideologies and concluding that there are defects and flaws in all of them. He even believed that democracy and freedom have their own problems. "There is no guaranty," he used to say, "that the majority will always make a correct decision, say in an election. What if a populist succeeded in exciting and motivating the majority of people by saying what they want to hear and presenting a manifesto to include what the excited mob see as their priorities and interests? Or what if the majority were illiterate and ignorant who could easily be cheated and manipulated?" They remembered him declaring, "I love and advocate freedom particularly freedom of speech and expressing one's view but, freedom without limit and without law attached to it; can lead to chaos and can be damaging to the community. One should not be allowed to say whatever he wants and insult other people's religion or principle, in the name or excuse of freedom of speech. Freedom in every aspects of the life, whether it is speech, expressing one's opinion, religious belief, political ideology, business or even life style ought to be within limits. Freedom must be protected and at the same time regulated by the law. Suppressing the freedom of people by autocrats is as wrong as absolute reckless freedom advocated by liberals. In defining the freedom we already have one rule and that is to say; you are free providing your free act doesn't prevent or endanger other people's freedom. We should accept more limitations and law around it to prevent anarchy. Unrestrained society is a real danger for people of any country and had to be prevented". His former classmates, who by then were practicing as lawyers, remembered him studying and investigating to find a fair system of governing the people and now that he had become king, they were sure that he was targeting that goal. The more they talked about their university friend and remembered of him the more they were hopeful for the major steps that he would take towards democracy.

While young king was waiting for referendum and its result he focussed on domestic matters too. He invited Colonel's family for dinner in palace and was delighted to see his angel Enzel who was now a young lady and his rescuer; Dr Ravid, who had qualified from medical school and was training to be a surgeon. He also asked Atta and his family to rent out their house and live in king's palace and appointed him as his personal advisor. He sent their children to best school in the city and provided the financial provisions for their future advanced educations by leaving enough money in their bank accounts; similar to the arrangement that he had done for his murdered friend's siblings. Atta was relatively well off and perhaps did not need financial support but was hugely grateful for the interest which king showed for securing his children's future education. When he was told about being appointed as king's personal advisor he was humbled and said, "Your majesty I am too insignificant person to be king's personal adviser."

"Can you stop calling me your majesty and call Alex please?"

"No your majesty, I cannot."

"Okay, as we agreed before; in private call me Alex and in public with official title."

"I'm sorry your majesty, I can't do that anymore. You are a king now and there is etiquette in relation to monarchs that we must follow." Alexander gave up the argument and talked about other matters including expecting him to be as useful to his son as he was for him when he was a child and teenager. Queen Tophia was over the moon now that she was reunited with her family but at times she felt that it was in dream that she is queen, not in reality. She felt; she was the luckiest woman in the world and was shocked to realize that how the act of a wicked person could lead to happiness of someone else. "Well, if God wants, it can happen." she said inside, "God saved the future king of our beautiful country and put me on his way, so that he notices me and then remembers seeing earlier in the university. Then we both fall in love and I become queen. I can't believe it but it must be true. I've even given birth to heir to the throne; it cannot all be in dream." She was shocked about the referendum as much as everyone else but she had heard of Alex enough in abroad to understand why this issue is his priority.

CHAPTER 15

The date for the referendum was announced by the government, and campaigns began with full fiscal support and provision of equal opportunities for both sides of the argument; republicans and monarchists. There was no discrimination as far as the access to the media was concerned and the coverages of their debates in radio and television. Of course, the newspapers took side depending whether they believed in monarchy or republic. King Alexander did not make any more comments and certainly did not wish to influence the people's decisions more than he had already done in his speech. Clearly he was more in favour of the republic even though did not regard any system without deficiencies. He encouraged more public debates and wide spread coverage of them in media to ensure that people make informed decision. The referendum under supervision of international observers was held and the surprising result was 80% in favour of monarchy. Alexander was very surprised with the result and said to Tophia, "I am sure love of people to my father influenced their decision. In spite of my advice they voted with their hearts not their brains. I thought republicans would win because they had better debates and campaign but surprisingly they did not win." Queen Tophia knew that Alexander's popularity among the people was a more important factor in their voting but did not dare to say so because she knew that her husband did not like being flattered. She was of course happy with the result as is expected from a queen but she knew Alexander would be happier; if lived as lawyer not king.

Late in the afternoon, the police chief and General Trojan came to see King Alexander and report events of the day after the result was announced.   Having been introduced to king by General Trojan police chief reported by saying, "Your majesty, since the result of referendum was announced there have been some scattered riots in the country."   Chief paused and then continued, "I am sorry to say that there have also been injuries to innocent by passers and damages to people's properties."

"Who are the rioters and what is their excuse for violence?" asked the king, "Is it the result of referendum that they object?

"Rioters are most likely gangs of anarchists assisted by the opportunists in hope of looting. Their objection of course is the result of referendum; claiming that it was manipulated."

"What the observers say?"

"They've declared no problem," said the chief, "in fact they have praised the government for organising the fairest and most flawless referendum. Republicans have formally accepted the result and distanced themselves from the rioters. " Young king facing with the first problem since succeeding his father thought for a few minute and said, "Broadcast a declaration in my name that although we respect the freedom of speech and expression of different views but we will not tolerate the violence or disturbance for public in the name of freedom. Therefore, perpetrators of the riot will be arrested and will remain in prison until they have fully paid for the repair of the damages done to properties and have paid acceptable compensation to the victims of their violence."   General Trojan and chief informed the king that, most of the leaders have already been identified and some of them have been arrested.   They then took their leave from king and left him with his thoughts. They were satisfied with the decision made.

Riot was fully controlled and main perpetrators were jailed. It was announced that the king will address the nation shortly to discuss the result of referendum. And the next day he did so.

*

"You have freely voted and overwhelming majority of you would like to continue with the monarchy. This is a democratic decision and all of us must respect it. But I still have some concerns about the constitution attached to the existing system. As I said in former speech; the existing constitution could potentially lead to dictatorship, in the hands of a wrong person I therefore suggest that it should be revisited and amended by the committee of experts that I have asked prime minister to convene. Members of the committee will be political leaders, judicial experts, relevant academics and legislatures from parliament selected by the MPs themselves. If you have any suggestion to this committee please write to them. I have some ideas that I share with you and will also write to that committee to be considered, if they found it worthy of consideration." He said it politely and smiled. In fact king Alexander was talking like a friend of people rather than a king; "There will be no specific order in my suggestions in this speech and I will simply mention them as come to my mind, although I will make it more orderly for the committee. Anyway, there should be a second House of Representatives in order to keep an eye on the work of our existing parliament (let us call it first house) and make sure that the legislations that pass through, are within constitutional laws and in the best interest of people. If the legislation does not meet the criteria they will return it to first House of Representatives for amendment. Second house will have no other power or function. The committee will determine the number of representatives in second house and details of relations between two houses. Unlike the first house in which all members are elected by the people I suggest in second house half of the representatives should be elected by people but, the other half should be appointed by king." He laughed and joked about giving power to himself but reassured the audience that they would soon appreciate the reason behind such a suggestion, which is about the balance of the power between the authorities. "After The general election the leader of the party with most MPs in the parliament will be appointed by the king as prime minster. But if king believed that the leader was not the right person for the post, he will appoint another MP from the same party to be prime minister   Prime minister will form the cabinet but each member of the cabinet should be accepted and approved by the parliament.   Whenever I say parliament I mean the first house. The parliament on behalf of the people; will have ultimate power.   They will have the right and authority to impeach and investigate the prime minister and any member of the cabinet and, remove them from the office; if they were found guilty of whatever had led to the impeachment.   They can also impeach the king and remove from the throne if was found guilty. And if that was the case they could either crown the heir to throne or decide differently.   I also propose that the parliament should have the power to call for a referendum whenever it was found in the interest of people.   For example in the case of king being removed from throne, if there was no suitable or legitimate successor; parliament could ask the government to convene another referendum to decide a different ruling system for the country. Equally, the king must have the power of dissolving the parliament and ordering general election if members of the houses and or government were not virtuous persons, were corrupted or were not working for welfare and interest of the nation.   All these measures and more which will be decided by the committee are for balance of the powers and safeguards to prevent any part of the ruling system to become dictator or corrupt.   Indeed all of us will be accountable before the nation. Constitution will make it clear that some impeachments could be triggered by the simple majority of MPs and others by absolute or special majority such as two third of MPs. As I have said before, although democracy and will of the majority is desirable but occasionally majority may make the wrong choice. That is precisely why education and health will be top priority for the government to make sure that there is no illiterate among us and we all enjoy reasonably healthy body and mind. To make sure that we are well-educated and well informed so that no one could mislead us when we go to the ballot box. Freedom of religious, political and social opinions should be an essential part of constitution and, must be protected by the law Freedom of speech, literature, art and the media ought to be included and protected too.   But I personally do not agree with the unrestrained freedom which could cause chaos, social disorder and disrespect to the others and could become an excuse in the hands of anarchists and hooligans to disturb the public and cause damages.   I would have wanted to expand this issue further if I was not conscious that I have already tired you too much.   So, I will leave it for some other time and only add here that on one hand I am sincere believer and defender of freedom and on the other hand very concerned about it; if it was not within limits and or was not attached to the law."

His friends (especially lawyers) who were eagerly listening to this speech, remembered him talking about the very subject in numerous occasions.   In debates about the freedom, he would purposely ask; do you mean that, one is free to steal properties of the other people, one is free to vandalise the public services, abuse a child, rape a woman and even is free to kill a human?   And when their answer was, "Of course not; law will not allow such conducts to happen or, if it happened will punish the perpetrator." Alex would go on with his questions to push the fanatic and passionate liberals into a corner. For example he would ask; does freedom allows you to produce films full of provocative pornography, violence, plundering and killing or raping and then, make it available for everyone including the children? Do you (by freedom of press) mean that you are free to abuse and insult other peoples' religions in your newspapers, journals and books or fabricate offensive stories about prominent figures of the society? By freedom, do you mean that you can insult and disgrace a politician, a religious leader or even an ordinary citizen in public for that matter? Of course not; and I could go on with other examples to get to the same answer from you. So clearly freedom has to be within limits and according to the law, belief and norms of the society.

*

The work of "special committee" continued for several months and the amended constitution was passed to the parliament for approval before putting it to yet another referendum. After some debates and in spite of reservation of certain sections of society, finally majority of the people voted yes to the amendment. But it did not satisfy everyone and peaceful protests began on streets. Protestors who were mainly in left side of political spectrum argued that, it is only a reform and the aim of the king is to prevent radical changes and revolution in the country.

CHAPTER 16

As a matter of fact amendment was comprehensive and quite radical.   The committee had included all of the king's proposals and had added many more, which were recommended by the political parties and various academics.   There was no loophole left in the law and it was almost impossible for any sections of the ruling system or any authority within the system to become corrupted or stablish dictatorship without being challenged, impeached and dismissed.   The ultimate power was in the hand of first House of Representatives (effectively; in the hands of people who had elected them), which would pass the legislations and could impeach the king as well as his government, if they moved away from constitutional laws, became corrupted or were inadequate in delivering their duties. Equally the king had the power of dismissing the government, dissolving the parliaments and ordering new general election, if he realized that they were not functioning in best interest of the people or had become corrupted. In other words each section of ruling system was keeping an eye on the others. Judicial system was totally independent and had the power of saying the last word, in any conflict or dispute between the powers. It was rather unexpected to have protestors on streets following such generous amendments. The main point of the protestors was that social injustice, poverty and inequality in society had not been solved by such a reform and only a revolution to stablish socialism would answer the problem. In his mind king knew that at least some of their points were correct and was hoping that the new parliament and government will be able to tackle those problems without revolution. In fact he thought what he had done was a revolution anyway.

As part of the freedom of speech and expression of one's opinion included in new constitution, such peaceful street demonstrations encountered no reaction or obstacles from the police side. But when the opportunists, far left radicals, far right extremists, hooligans and anarchists joined them, it became necessary for the authorities to intervene in order to stop the spread of disruption and vandalism. Like the previous occasion king and his government would not tolerate it and arrests were made.   Young king once again went on air to talk to people. This was in fact scheduled for a week after the result of referendum on constitution to inform the people about next steps that he had in mind but was brought forward; because of disorders in the country and rumours that some of royalists are preparing to confront with the protestors that, could have disastrous consequences.   After greetings the people of his country, king began his third speech since succeeding his father.   "On behalf of the great nation of this country, I would like to thank members of the committee for their honest, meticulous and professional hard works in amending the old constitution and thank you for voting yes for the new constitution. I do believe that, this is a major step toward the democracy and creating fairer society but of course, more must be done. That is precisely why some of our fellow countrymen and women began protesting in streets and telling that merely amending the constitution is not enough to tackle poverty and injustice in society. I sincerely thank them for the point they make and for doing it so peacefully.   That is what the freedom of speech and expression of view means and law will protect that right. But unfortunately once again anarchists and hooligans spoiled the party. This will not be tolerated, I promise. Perpetrators will be put in prison and will remain there until they are adequately rehabilitated, learned the true meaning of freedom and compensate all the damages done to the public. I am told some of these hooligans who were arrested in previous occasion are still in prison. Well,

they can stay there for as long as they wish. We will not neglect security and wellbeing of our people in this country. Appropriate legislations will make it clear what are permissible in our society and what are not. We are all free within limits of the laws and the laws will be based on religious belief of this nation, moral standards and norms of the society. There are certain rights that even law cannot take it from you. We are free to choose our own religions and worship in relevant holy places, without being disturbed or harassed and all the religions are free
in this country; protected by the law. We are free to believe in any political ideology and be active in spreading our ideas peacefully through all sorts of publications, meetings or lectures etcetera. All political parties are free whether royalists, conservatives, democrats, liberals or socialists. But of course no racism or fascism will be tolerated or allowed in our land to join political activities simply because dictatorship is imbedded within their ideology which the whole idea of new constitution is to prevent it happening. Freedom of speech is also one of the rights that no one could take away from us but it should not be misunderstood. It does not mean that we are free to utter whatever comes to our minds, no matter how unfair, offensive or untrue it is and how insulting it might be to other people. I must confess that when it comes to the subject of freedom, I go on talking; not only about my passionate belief in freedom of humans but also about my worries; if it was unrestrained freedom and if it was not within the limits of law. However, I better stop here and talk about other matters."

His former university friends knew this very well as many times he had debated with them and challenged fanatic liberals. He believed that freedom of people except for the ones which he had mentioned in his speeches; varies from society to society. For example usage of the drugs or its distribution might be free in one country and forbidden in another and citizens ought to recognize that if law does not allow then they are not free to engage in using them or distributing. And he would give numerous similar examples such as being gay, gay marriage, nudity, whoredom etcetera. He was concerned about misunderstanding of freedom or making it as an excuse to do mischiefs as hooligans, opportunists and some of the so called critics do. Another example of misunderstood version or deliberately using it for own interests which he would frequently mention; was freedom of the press where, just to sell their papers they make fabricated stories and accusations against certain individuals whether politicians or celebrities and even innocent ordinary people and leave them disgraced in public eyes. He did not agree with any type of freedom that could be harmful to people particularly children whom had no experience to distinguish right from wrong or good from bad.

"He even was against the provocative attire and appearance of females in public," declared a friend jokingly, "and love making in public."

"Or publishing misleading materials in books and media or producing films, videos that directly or indirectly teaches and advocates socially unacceptable behaviour, violence, killing and all sorts of crimes," said another one more seriously.

"Sometimes such opinions and comments appear in contrast with his passionate support of freedom," said a concerned friend, "and this might cause problem for him. But we know he is very clear in one thing; freedom within law and you can't argue about that."

"I think his harsh words against far right as well as fanatic liberals are more likely to cause problem for him." Another friend added.

King continued his speech by returning to protestors, "I agree with your concerns. Yes, we should do much more in public services, provision of affordable health and education, raising the minimum wage and in essence eliminating poverty in our relatively affluent country. The term of existing parliament is coming to an end in a couple of months' time. All political parties should nominate their candidates and begin campaigning in favour of their thoughts as well as their plans if they win the general election. Let me specifically address the socialists and communists; if you really believe that your ideas would create a fairer and happier society or as you say will guarantee the social justice then, please explain it more clearly to the nation and if majority voted for you, form the government and serve your fellow countrymen and women.   When you have this opportunity, why choose violence, why bloodshed? If majority think as you do then surely you will win the election in democratic way but if not, why a minority should rule on the nation by force? Don't you agree with democracy?   Sometimes I wonder whether you do, when I read about dictatorship of the proletariat in your books."   Here king changed the subject again and talked about other matter and finally; encouraged the people to listen to all sides of the debates and vote to the candidates or parties which they think will protect their interests and work for the happiness of the nation. He said, queen and I have two votes and will certainly come to ballot box like everyone else. He then wished good luck for everyone and asked the government to make certain that both voting and counting the votes are flawless.

In the meantime, many hooligans were arrested and street protests gradually decreased and stopped.   Parties began preparing for the general election of both parliaments while the king's loyal prime minister and his beloved head of the army continued with their duties, waiting for the result of election and formation of new government.

CHAPTER 17

General election started and people enthusiastically queued for long hours to vote. Polling stations were guarded by the police and to begin with there were no disturbances to repot. But early in the afternoon, the far right activists and anarchists who were angry with the arrests of their comrades; began rioting again and made voting in certain areas rather difficult. Although such unrests were reported to king but against the advice of prime minster and his chief of security he decided to join ordinary people in one of the station in order to vote. So, together with queen and while surrounded by body guards and security officers they went to a polling station not too far from the palace and voted. The news of king and queen voting alongside the ordinary voters spread rapidly and outside the polling station many people gathered to see them. King ignoring the anxiety of officers for his safety began talking to people lovingly. It did not take too long before concerns of the security staff was proved valid. A shot was fired and king fell on the ground, bleeding.

There was a chaos in the scene; queen was screaming and weeping while kneeled beside king's body, police and guards were trying to release the suspect from the hands of angry people, who had arrested him and were beating relentlessly while the rest of people had left the queue were tying to help but did not how. Someone was shouting, "Call for ambulance" the other, "Bring the first aid box" and another, "Let me in, I am a doctor". Bleeding was heavy from chest but king was conscious trying to calm the queen, "Don't worry it is a mild injury, we just need to stop the bleeding."

Doctor managed to stop heavy bleeding but was concerned about the amount of blood lost. He hoped there will be blood or blood component available in the ambulance in order to start transfusion before transferring the patient but there were none and so king was rushed to hospital. Queen was not allowed to go and was taken back to palace but doctor accompanied the king. In hospital blood transfusion commenced immediately and surgeon performed the necessary operation. He then informed the prime minister and General Trojan who by then had arrived with alarm; that, the bullet had not entered inside the lung and was trapped between the muscle and bone. He reassured them that there was no danger to king's life but at present he will remain in the recovery room and could not be visited yet. "As my party participates in election," said the prime minister to General, "I don't want to interfere in the procedures. I wonder if you could kindly talk to the nation through radio and television, to let them know of this terrible incident and reassure that, there is no danger to his majesty's life. Please encourage the people to continue voting in peace and if you think it is necessary; allow the time of voting to be extended."

"I will do it with pleasure. Thank God king escaped from this assassination too."

"Yes, it would be a real tragedy if assassin had succeeded. But his majesty must learn the lesson that, he and his family need protection round the clock and listen to what security staff advice."

Queen Tophia, queen mother and Colonel Poxon (now a one star general) came to see king as soon as doctors allowed. Tophia was crying again but this time with joy that her love was alive. Queen mother who had fainted when she heard the news was not able to control herself either. King smiled at them and said, "It is nothing, I am sure doctor will discharge me soon. Well," he added jokingly, "This is the second time they fail; they might be lucky third time."

*

The result of election expectedly was in favour of Royalist Party. They had clear majority in parliament to form the government. King appointed the leader of the party as prime minister and he soon presented his cabinet to first House of Representatives for approval. Departed king's loyal prime minister wished to be retired but king persuaded him to serve in the second house and put his name amongst the appointed members of that parliament. He also asked Trojan to remain as commander in chief. And when he was informed that the young man who had tried to kill him; was not connected to any party or organisation, king wished to meet and talk to him and this was arranged.

"Why did you want to see me dead?" King asked the young man after offering him a chair to sit. He was a tall thin lad who sat indifferently as if sitting beside a person equal to himself.

"I don't know." He answered.

"Have I done anything wrong to you or your family?"

"No."

"But there must be a reason behind such a terrible thing to do. Getting hold of a gun and finding out where I will be at that time; requires some planning and perhaps assistance too."

"I already had the gun and wanted to commit suicide. No one else is involved. It was pure accident that I learned where you were going to vote."

"So, very wisely decided to kill a king rather than yourself, is that so?"

"You could say so, but that was not the reason. I was just angry and depressed. For some years I've been angry with the injustice in society, with inequality and misery of my life. I am very poor and you are too rich, I've no house and you have too many houses and palaces, I've no job when you are a king and could be a lawyer, if you were not the king. I could not afford to go to university and you did afford, not only in this country but abroad too. It is not fair."

"I understand what you say but, do you really think if I was killed, you could have all these that you were deprived of?"

"No."

"You found me obvious example of inequality in our country and a symbol of injustice but do you really think by eliminating one example, equality would be instantly established in the society and justice will prevail?"

"No sir. I now realize that it is a stupid way of solving the problem. I just did it at the height my anger and frustration without thinking. I have committed an unforgivable crime and will not be able to look at the eyes of people who adore you. I deserve punishment and I am prepared for it." King looked at him with mixture of affection and sadness and after a pause asked, "You said you don't have home. Where do you stay then?"

"I stay in prison."

"I meant before that."

"Occasionally I stayed with my poor parents, sometimes with friends but most of the times I slept in the streets or parks."

"What about money?"

"I have unemployment allowance." King thought for some time and then called the prison officer who had brought the young man and told him; "I have no complain against this young man. Inform whoever has the authority, to release him and transfer to a residential training centre to be trained in whatever job he is interested at. His unemployment benefit should stop and he should be paid for training and working in that centre not less than standard minimum wage."

Young man could not believe his ears and eyes. Officer escorted him out of the room and king called his secretary. "I want to see prime minister," he said, "could you arrange it?" He then called her back and added, "Tell him it is not urgent, he can come whenever he is free." This was arranged and king met the prime minister. He informed him about pardoning the assassin and requesting the authorities to send him to residential training centre. He talked about his idea that, unemployment benefit should only be given to those that, because of their physical or mental disabilities are incapable of working. Unemployment benefit of those who are healthy and can work must be stopped and all of them should be trained for the skills that country needs and for the jobs that they wish to have later on.   They should be paid while are working and learning in training centres and this mentality of living on the benefit ought to be changed to self-esteem and mentality of living with dignity and proud life.

"I am not interfering in your job prime minister," concluded the king, "but I wonder if you would consider the appropriate legislations, in relation to the unemployment allowance, as well as the nationwide training for all the individuals who are healthy but prefer not to work or genuinely cannot find a job.   We will of course need huge budget in order to increase the number of residential and non-residential training centres throughout the country and pay for the trainers as well as the trainees but I 'm sure the industrialists would help because, it is in their interests too; to produce skilled workers at home rather than importing them from other countries."   He then talked about tghe inequality in society and the fact that gap between poor and rich is shameful and unsustainable. Leader of Royalist Party, now prime minister, was surprised to hear king's views that would be music to the ears of socialists. In fact his university friends had always commented on this point in their political and philosophical debates that his ideas are close to socialism.

"I am sure you would consider passing legislations," king continued with his ideas, "to tax the high income earners and wealthy people more; in order to pay for the cost of better health service, free education and training schemes."   After some further discussions prime minister promised king that his government would work hard for better public service, for tackling the poverty and reducing the gap between poor and rich.   When he was taking his leave king jokingly said, "Don't worry I am not going to govern the country. I assure you I will stick to my duties as stated in constitution.   But seriously speaking, you should welcome the ideas that are thrown to you by public or oppositions."   Prime minister acknowledged his appreciation and left the king with his thoughts. And king decided to talk to nation again and asked chief of his staff to arrange it. "I will not bother people too often," he said inside, "but I think this is important after what happened and the amount of love and well wishes that they showed." This talk was arranged for the following week. In the meantime he thought about his vision for the future of his country. If there was only one thing that he would wholeheartedly agree with the socialists and communists; that was the ugliness and unfairness of the poverty in any country, let alone in their affluent land. Indeed it was the existence of inequality and social injustice in country that had made him so concerned since was a young student. Now he had inherited vast amount of wealth from his father and was not comfortable about it at all. So, he donated more than half of his fortune to the government to be used for the training, health and education and hoped other affluent persons in the country will do the same. He transferred all of the antiques and works of the art from both palaces to the national museum and passed the ownership of second palace (where occasionally he and most of the times, his brother used to live) to the government; to be used as residence for the prime ministers and working place for the cabinet ministers. The time for addressing the nation arrived and in his speech he referred to some of his ideas but there was no mention about above mentioned genericities.

CHAPTER 18

"Truly, I cannot thank you enough," said the king after warm greetings to the nation, "for your prayers and compassionate words and well wishes in recent days and weeks." He did not say anything about the association attempt against his life, subsequent hospital admission and the operation he underwent. Instead, he talked about the election results and formation of new government. "Thank God we now have your representatives in both houses," said he, "and new government has begun its service to people. Prime minister has informed me that very soon appropriate legislations will be presented to the parliaments; aiming to eliminate poverty in our country and establish fairer society and indisputable social justice. By no means could anyone say that we totally lacked these privileges, far from it. But more reforms are necessary following my father's hard work, for so many years. The great king moved this country, from absolute dictatorship towards democracy and made this society a safer and fairer place to live in compared with what it was decades ago. Now, with the new constitution, efforts of your representatives and honest service of the new government; the ultimate ambitions of that great man will be attained." As if he had no role in any changes since he succeeded his father he continued praising the beloved father, his chosen prime minister and other former officials for the great work they had done and their undeniable achievements but at the same time acknowledged that more works are necessary to complete their efforts and get this country where the great king had meant to take. "I'm glad to learn," he continued, "that one of many projects which new administration will pursue, is nationwide training for all the unemployed people, who are capable of working. It is good to hear that this mentality or habit of living on benefits or allowances is going to be changed. Obviously, we must continue supporting our fellow countrymen and women who are not able to work. You will appreciate that having training centres throughout the country together with objectives such as having best health service and free education at all levels for all, require massive budget and manpower. I trust our businessmen and women, industrialists and universities would help in providing the trainers and those of us who have been fortunate to be well off will generously and willingly contribute to cost of these schemes over and above paying tax according to the law. I am also sure that the upper class realizes that, the gap between poor and rich is unsustainable and there is no reason for the violence when we can change it to better in peaceful way. I call on those who are on the left of political spectrum and sincerely advise them to follow democratic means to attain their goals and distance themselves from hooligans and anarchists. There is no need for bloodshed when democratic ways are open for you. In future elections, if majority of people supported your ideas you will form the government and the constitution even allows you to run a further referendum to change the system, if people of this country saw more appropriate at the time. I also address the affluent section of society and expect them to fully comprehend what I mean and assist the government; to put an end to injustice in our society." This was very tough talk from a king and his university friends who were keenly listening to his speech genuinely worried for him.

"He is going too fast," said one of the friends, "making enemies from all sides."

"Yes," said the other, "far right and left will not like the language he uses and plans he has in mind. Wealthy people will neither like what he is cooking for them nor give up their riches and positions so easily."

"Don't forget that he has support of the people." Said the

third one but others dismissed that optimism on the ground that people can easily be persuaded to change sides. Alarmed friends made occasional comments while listening to king. And king continued pouring out his ideas and expressing his hopes for the people amongst whom he had grown up and was familiar with their sufferings, pains and sorrows as well as their desires and hopes for their children.   "My young brothers and sisters," said he, "allow me to advise you on education. Pursue higher education in variety of fields particularly in science. Some of you should go abroad to learn from other nations' achievements.   Some of you should become fluent in foreign languages of advanced nations; in order to translate their scientific books and essays to our language and ours to theirs, so that, we all learn from each other and neither we nor anyone else are left behind."   Here he jokingly said if you learn their language properly, they will not be able to cheat us in treaties, by adding ambiguous words or phrases in small prints. He then went on talking about serious matters and his dream of a time that there will be no more wars on planet earth and all nations will happily live in peace. Human will grow in knowledge, moral maturity and spiritual development towards the perfection.   "I wish there was always peace between the nations so that; all the efforts and resources of humankind were spent for discovering the wonders of life and majesty of the universe."   He talked about using the natural resources and wealth of the country for providing the happy and healthy life for all rather than spending for arms to kill the fellow humans.But unfortunately that was only a dream and he knew the bitter reality of human history which is saturated by all sorts of crimes, aggression of one nation against the other, wars and genocide. "I grieve to admit that," he continued, "we cannot invest on such dreams and optimism and have to build up our defence too.   I say defence because we will never invade another country.   Government will arrange peace treaties with our neighbours and will not fall in the trap of arms race that big powers force upon other countries." And he went on explaining how the superpowers create wars to sell their weapons to those who are engaged in the wars and sponsor terrorism to cause fear amongst public to have excuse for more wars and more arms trades. Having talked about all legal and illegal arms trades and how super-powers' existence at least partially depends on sale of arms to rich but under developed countries he promised that, newly elected government will not waste the money to gratify them. Finally he said, "I will strictly observe my role and en-titlements within the constitution and will not intervene in running day to day affairs of the country. That is prime min-ister's responsibility and role but, I will certainly keep a close eye on function of your representatives, our government and various institutions to make sure that peoples' rights and interest are protected and all of us consider ourselves servants of this nation and work for you rather than our personal inter-ests. I will not bother you too often with my speeches ex-cept for in certain occasions or whenever government wants me to do so. God bless you all." And so, he ended one more ma-jor speech for the delight of his admirers.

"It was not enough to make enemies within" said one of the lawyers, "he challenged the big powers outside too, to com-plete the range of enemies."

"He hasn't and will never change." Another friend re-marked, "I really worry very much that unlike what he just promised; he will continue pushing the government to imple-ment his projects, forgetting that ruling party is founded by very wealthy and influential people, who will not like radical changes."

"Will far left be happy with mere reforms; of course not." concluded another worried friend, "They want revolution and they believe "proletarian dictatorship" is true democ-racy, not the type of democracy that he is advocating. Will far right be happy with what he is talking about, again of course not? Racism is in their blood. They cannot even imagine that white skin is not superior to dark or, all the religions ought to be free, respected and protected by law. Are we all equal? You must be joking. Will the upper class and affluent people give up some of their money so easily for public services, for free health and education? Will they not try to protect their social status and influence? Yes, they are all royalists but until king is with them not when he acts against their interests." "Add super powers to the list," said a lawyer, "who will not be happy either. Should we warn him? Yes of course. Will he listen? No." But they decided to warn him anyway.

CHAPTER 19

Seven years later what the king's friends were worried about; happened. The first three years all went very well. Parliament passed legislation to increase the tax for high income earners and rich people. The minimum wage was increased substantially. Even though reluctantly; but nevertheless wealthy persons donated generous sums of money to be spent for public services. Of course, they did so after king had donated most of what he inherited from father, for the same purpose. Nationwide training was very successful to the delight of industrialists and young unemployed people. Education and health services became free for all. Transport, communications, energy and all natural resources were nationalised and king with the support of fans and his influence on officials of the government continued to move towards the targets which were fairness and justice in country. Of course, well off families were not happy at all about the amount of the tax that they were paying and those on right or left of the political spectrum were not pleased with the reforms either (for different logic of course)' but there were no troubles in the country except for sporadic protests or minor riots on the streets.

During the same period of time, government managed to sign commercial contracts and peace treaties with neighbouring countries. Purchasing the weapons from gigantic cartels and various manufacturers of the big countries was stopped and all weapons (for the purpose of defence) were manufactured by the nation's own engineers and workers.This together with the nationalisation of natural resources, especially oil; were not pleasant news for the domineering powers outside the country, who had robbed the underdeveloped and developing countries for centuries.   And downfall of the system which king had stablished; began for that very fact. There was another factor that worried the imperialists in western world and that was the spread of king's ideas in other countries of that region. Those powerful states who still had imperialistic mentalities and very much wished to continue with their influence on weaker countries (while stealing their natural resources) could not bear true democracy and independence. Of course they always seemed to advocate democracy and freedom as a whole, and free elections in particular. But they would only be happy about the outcomes, if their own puppets were elected.

However, time was approaching fast for the second general election, since the approval of new constitution and parties had already begun campaigning.   Socialist party was very active this round and it seemed that, people were more supportive of them perhaps because they felt that king's ideas are closer to that party than any other party including royalists.

The result of election became a real nightmare for the western powers because, not only socialists had more members of parliament this round but even the communists had succeeded in taking some seats.   Although the royalist had more seats than any other party but they no longer enjoyed absolute majority and had to either form a minority government or have coalition with left which they chose the second option. With such coalition country moved more rapidly towards the left and that was what the big powers worried about a great deal and they began causing problems.

First they encouraged and assisted one of the neighbouring countries to invade part of the land and war was forced upon king who had wished peace for all counties in the world.

With the force of navy already present in the area they blocked export of the oil which was country's main source of income and also, interrupted the imports too.   Then secret agents of a superpower, assassinated General Trojan and his deputy became commander in chief with the approval of king. He was not known to the king personally and he merely approved the decision because he trusted Trojan in choosing the right person as his deputy. This turned out to be a big mistake as secret services of big powers easily bought him for their plans.

To begin with, they brought the hooligans and anarchists (who had no specific ideology), into the cities to cause further disorders in the middle of war. Encouraged by the foreign currency in their pockets, which was passed to them by agents of superpowers; they did all the damages possible to the public services and private properties. And once the people were weary of the unrests, riots, insecurities, heavy casualties of the war and shortages of foods and basic necessities of their daily lives; the functioning powers from outside, signalled to their already recruited officers in the army to seize the power. Following the successful military coup the parliaments were closed and all senior members of the government were arrested. Few officers who were known to be loyal to the king, including Tophia's father General Poxon, were put in prison too. Immediately afterwards; with the signal of big brother war stopped and crackdown on the opposition began mercilessly. Many leaders or high rank members of Socialist and Communist parties were arrested and some of them were executed. Then political activities of all parties, except for the pro west Republicans, who had assisted the coup, were banned and media was restricted. King was in house arrest and nation was in shock and disbelief. King, having faced with such an unexpected tragedy, was devastated as all his and the peoples' achievements had been thrown away. Now, by Trojan being killed and most of the officials being in jail or executed he had no help and there seemed not much options available to act upon. However, with the help of Atta the only ally left for him he managed to communicate with his people through the letters and recorded speeches hoping they will show resistance and regain their independence and freedom.   In fact they came to streets; to regain their stolen democracy but this led to a fierce reaction from the ruling generals with more killing and imprisonments and king very much regretted to have encouraged the people to rise against dictatorship.   Brutality of police and army was unbelievable and outside the world did not remain silent but with no effect.   Inside the country, it was heading to a full civil war, which would affect the whole region and this was neither in the interest and plans of grief-stricken king nor was what the generals and their supporting big brother wanted.   However, as the powers behind the military coup, had achieved all their objectives, they advised the governing generals to negotiate with king to calm down the situation. They did not want further trouble in that sensitive region and compromised agreement with the king seemed more desirable. They were also concerned about the popularity of king amongst the nation and possibility of future uprisings.   The commander in chief that was now head of the military government did not dare (or, perhaps was too ashamed to meet the king) and therefore, he sent a team to negotiate. They came to the palace, respectfully met the king and explained the situation together with available options.   They made it clear that they could simply continue killing the protestors or putting them in prison for as long as it takes in order to put an end to any resistance whether now or in future.   Between the lines they made king to understand that, they could easily kill him too if that was the only option left for them. King already knew all these and the fact that; one particular superpower behind the coup, has so much interest in the region that will do any crime to protect it.   History had also taught him the bitter fact that in such situations the other superpower in eastern world, minds his own business and is more anxious about protecting his own interests than trying to intervene or support any oppressed nation.   He was also aware that United Nations had done nothing about his government's complaint, (when the country was invaded) and surely now that war was over it was unlikely that such an institution that practically is a toy in the hands of superpowers would do anything about the coup. UN had already ignored the sanctions imposed by one country, without the approval of the Security Council. Above all he did not want any more bloodshed.   Therefore, he too was hoping to gain something from the negotiation and listened carefully to what representatives of military government were telling or hinting.   Negotiation went on for a long time and at the end representatives of generals agreed to release all the ordinary prisoners and General Poxon but no other officials or leaders of the parties for the time being. They agreed to open the parliaments and allow the members to work as normal but of course for the present military government. They did not say that their boss will lift the sanctions as soon as resistance stopped, but king knew it will happen and that was important for welfare of the public. In return king offered to abdicate when the system will automatically change to republic; based on a clause in included in the constitution. He promised to advise the nation to stop fighting that had continued since coup and advice the fanatic royalists to be patient and accept the changes. All this providing they promise to hold free election to choose president under the supervision of observers from UN. He also requested an opportunity to talk to people via radio and television.   Generals' negotiators were prepared to promise an election for presidency within six months but, they were very concerned about the live broadcast of his speech, which was what he did want.   Since king did not agree that a censured and distorted speech of him to be broadcasted and because it was vital for military government to come out of the unpredictable situation, they had to accept it and the king talked to people for the last time.

*

"Truly I cannot adequately express my deep grief and profound regret for what has happened to our young democracy. I never thought anyone of our countrymen or women would sell their country to those foreign oppressors, to those evils that have sucked the blood of poor nations for decades if not centuries. But they sold their country and betrayed the nation for personal gains, power, position and money.   It is very sad indeed. Sadder still, is the reality that, western powers or to be precise that blood thirsty superpower behind this coup, are too powerful for us to fight with.   I am deeply grieved for many lives which have been lost during the imposed war and since the traitors' coup. I'm sorry for all the tortures and imprisonments of innocent people.   Truly I feel responsible for all these sufferings.   My father asked your forgiveness for his errors that in my view were minor faults, but I do not deserve forgiveness and I don't ask it.   Perhaps after General Trojan's assassination by the agents of that wicked superpower I should have taken the responsibility of commander in chief myself as is stated in constitution rather than replacing his deputy to such position whom so easily fell in the trap of foreign powers.   Perhaps in this way, I would have put loyal royalists in sensitive posts and this calamity would not have happened. Or perhaps we should not have reformed so radically which frightened the enemies." He did not say that, perhaps we should not have nationalised the oil industry; knowing that how desperate the western powers are to control the oil fields and its export.   But he continued by saying, "I ask you to stop the resistance for the time being to see whether what they have promised me will be honoured or not. Please go to your families and let us mourn for loss of our loved ones in peace.   I also ask the army personnel to return to their garrisons and stop murdering and harassing their brothers and sisters.   Military government has promised me to release all prisoners immediately except for some of the senior officers and members of our lawful government but I hope they too will soon be released.   The parliaments will open and MPs will resume their work." He hesitated to announce his decision to abdicate because he knew that it would be much unexpected for the people to hear but he had made his mind and so after a long pause he went on to say, "My dear friends, I hereby announce my abdication with immediate effect.　The system in this country will change to republic as new constitution has foreseen it.　In the circumstances such as this one, parliament can approve the change and there is no need for referendum. I ask all royalists to accept the change and continue their efforts to protect the democracy as far as possible. With all respect; I ask members of the parliaments to approve the change of system and once again amend the constitution that I guess will be mainly removing the parts related to king or replacing them with president. I must say that in the referendum, I voted for republic but once majority chose monarchy, we did all we could to construct a mixture of the both systems.　In fact what we achieved would have been the fairest system of governing the country, if they had allowed us to live in peace.　However, I had a meeting with generals; they have accepted to hold a free election for the presidency, within six months that will be observed by the observers from UN. I don't know how an election could be free if parties are not allowed to campaign and the leaders are in prison. I do hope that they would think about it seriously and free them all, well before election date.　I remain hopeful that perhaps all is not lost. We are now an educated and a well-informed nation.　This generation and surely next generations will not allow the return of dictatorship. I advise the military government to honour the terms of our agreement in recent meeting and trust they will.　But if they did not respect, I myself will come to the streets to fight against them alongside brave people and I believe most of the army personnel and police would join us, as the enemy could not have bought all of them."

King appeared very emotional and sad.　Tears in his eyes, he talked for another couple of minutes that was mainly saying farewell to the nation.　People were left astonished, grieved and some bitterly felt abandoned. Minority of people saw his decision as betrayal, but majority took it as the ultimate sacrifice of their beloved king who equally loved them. His university friends knew him too well to be surprised of his decision but felt very sorry that all his achievements appeared to have been stolen. "Yes," said one of the friends, "it has been stolen precisely by the same powers, which he always criticised and hated as the main source and cause of the sufferings and unhappiness amongst the nations." "We must go and see him," suggested the other, "he must feel lonely, sad and depressed." They all agreed and sent message to him. In the meantime, like the message from last speech of king, they too were optimistic about the future.

*

Soon after king's speech sporadic protests and fighting stopped and most of prisoners were released. The parliaments were opened, sanctions and embargo were lifted. King went to live with his parents in law and left the palace to Atta. He instructed him to continue living with his family in the same apartment of the palace as before but to open the rest of it to public to visit freely or with small entrance fee in order to cover the cost of maintenance of the palace. Generals honoured the agreement and election was held six months later and leader of Republic Party was elected as president; of course with blessing of the big brother. Abdicated king called the elected president to congratulate and asked him to free the rest of prisoners and work towards the national reconciliation. He hoped that other parties will be allowed to be active and future will be bright for people. On the personal ground; he found it almost impossible and certainly impractical to work as lawyer in his own country, live and be treated as an ordinary person. Therefore, he reluctantly went to exile in the same country that he had obtained his PhD.

RESEMBLANCE

CHAPTER 1

Early morning, on a spring day in London, a young man left his noisy flat hoping to find a quiet place in order to sit down and think carefully. Streets of London were too crowded and too noisy for him; who had just escaped from that very nuisance. He desperately needed a quiet location with no distraction around, so that he could focus on the various factors before him and come up with the correct decision and choice. He was in his late twenties, a handsome man with above average height, white skin, dark brown hair and black eyes. He was not presumed British by birth, but had lived and worked in the United Kingdom for more than eleven y ears. During those years he had successfully completed the medical course in Cambridge Medical School and postgraduate training in London hospitals, leading to surgery. He was granted permanent visa to remain in that country, if he adopted her as his new home; which in fact he wished to do so. The results of all of his exams were marked "passed with distinction" and all of his diplomas were granted to him with "honours". His exceptional talents had attracted the attention of many influential senior medical staff in the country. One of eminent professor had offered him the sub-speciality training for "neuro-surgery", in his own department at senior registrar level and the other had offered to send him to United States for the same sub-speciality training. They knew that his ambition was to be a neurosurgeon. To make the decision even more difficult, he had also received an offer of "university post" from his native country.

He reached to the Kensington Park but was disappointed

to find it full of the people who were sunbathing, eating, drinking, dancing, playing different games and making a lot of noise from, which he had escaped. It was a sunny day and hot weather, unusual for the first week of March and typically people wanted to make most of it. "I don't blame them," he said inside, "we don't often have such a pleasant weather." Unlike some people he liked unpredictability of the weather in this country and jokingly would say; "There are no real and separate seasons as we know of and I love constant changes in the weather here. You don't get bored with one type of weather. You could have hot weather for few days in the middle of winter and freezing cold in the middle of summer. You can have stormy wind in the middle of night, rain in the morning, sunshine in the afternoon and blustery shower at night. It has always been like that. Look at the old and new photos; the British gentleman always carries an umbrella even if the rain is not forecasted." He passed through the crowd to find a cooler and quitter corner but all shaded areas under all the big trees had already been taken by the families with young children, in order to protect them as well as the old ones from the sun burn and the excessive heat. Everywhere else was packed with the sun lovers in various activities. He kept changing his direction in the park searching for a suitable place and having failed to find what he wanted; began thinking about his position and calculating the issue in hand, while wondering around unintentionally.

The offer for United States was a unique opportunity for him; as the centre in which he would have been trained (had he chosen that option) was the best in the world with state of the art equipment and facilities. The main negative point about such option was far distance from his home land (or more precisely from his mother whom he loved more than anything in his life). And of course he also had to leave all the friends he had made over years living in the United Kingdom. The eminent professor's offer of training him in his own department would have eliminated those negative points, which he had created in his mind, but his emotional state was an obstacle to accept that either so easily.   Separation from his mother had become too long now and the last time he saw her (when he returned home for funeral of his father) he utterly felt guilty of not having any share in looking after and caring for mother. Father had left houses, land and plenty of money for his family.   So, mother was quite comfortable both from financial point of view and with the servants to attend her needs but, loneliness was bothering her and, he knew well that all his siblings were busy with their jobs and their young families. When he informed his mother of the opportunities that he was offered in UK and USA she had answered, "Do what is best for you my son. Don't think about me."   But when he was returning to UK, his mother with tears in her eyes and a broken voice had said; come back, I miss you a lot. I've tolerated this for more than ten years. I can't anymore; now that your father is gone.   "Emotionally, that is what my mother wishes," he thought, "but when the other day she said (do whatever is best for you) it was her usual sacrifice." Returning home and taking university post obviously had some advantages. He could stay with mother, love her, take care of her and compensate the past neglects that he truly felt ashamed for.   He could also begin teaching in Medical schools, open his private practice and serve the people of his country who needed him more than his would be adopted country. "But again," he said inside, "why not to do such service in a better position after becoming neurosurgeon, as there are very few of them at home." He tried to put emotion aside and think practically. "Mother can wait for another few years," he reassured himself inside, "and I could go and see her more often than before or, if she accepts, I can bring her to UK to live with me."   He was wondering around in the park aimlessly and thinking about all these matters, repeating the arguments for and against each option. He was lost in his thoughts and did not have any idea about his whereabouts.   He did not know whether he was still in Kensington Park, Hyde Park or outside the parks, when he suddenly found himself in front of a magnificent house. This took him back to his childhood. The architecture of house was Eastern style and reminded him of his father's house. Through the gate of house he could see a big garden, a pool in the middle and huge rectangular flower beds either side of it and balconies facing the garden. He was miles away when he heard the horn of a car and voice of the driver asking him to move aside. He was in the middle of the driveway, blocking the way of a Roles-Royse with the chauffeur behind the wheel and, two ladies in the back seat.   He apologised and began moving away from the car and house, when an old lady shouted from inside of the car, "Please stop. Don't go. Please wait." Then with the help of her driver, she got out of the car and while limping with obvious agony; hurried towards the young man with indescribable joy and excitement shouting "I've found him, I have found my grandson."

"I am not your grandson madam," said the young man, "you are mistaking."

"There can be no mistake; you are exactly like your grandfather. Tell me where they say you were borne."

"Azerbaijan."   As soon as this was uttered, the old lady screamed with joy and was about to fall on her back when the young man caught her in the middle of the air and gently laid her on the floor while using palm of his hand as a cushion to protect the head.   Meanwhile a young lady got out of the car shouting, "What happened grandma?"

"Don't worry; she just fainted," said he, "She will be alright in a minute." Without taking any notice of that verdict, the young lady began examining the patient and once she had finished said, "Wake up grandma you are okay." She then turned to the young man and asked, "What did you tell her?"

"She asked where was I born and I just said where, that is all." The old lady was just about to come around when two female servants arrived with a wheelchair and gently put her in and transferred back into the car. A police who had witnessed the event said, "Shall I call for ambulance?"   No, was the answer from the young lady. Once again the young man began to walk away but soon the policeman called him back and began questioning; "Why were you looking inside the house?"

"The architecture fascinated me. It reminds me of my childhood."

"Really?" said the policeman sarcastically, "what are you doing here in the first place? This is a private residential area and you are a stranger."

"I really don't know. I was walking in the Kennington Park but suddenly found myself in front of this house."

"Is that so? Said the police with obvious suspicion, "And if you were not interrupted by their arrival, you would have gone inside to see what else in this house could interest you. Am I right?"

"No, you are mistaking. I am not a burglar, I am a doctor." While saying so he showed his hospital ID card.

"Okay you are one of those foreign junior doctors. It makes no difference here." said the police with hatred and disgust evident in his voice and body language. The young man had a lot of admirations for the country and her ordinary people but, was worried about racism and the fact that; no matter how long you lived in that country, you are still a foreigner. And this was one of the reasons why he had not yet formally chosen her as his adopted country.

"I'm not convinced with your explanation," police continued, "you must come with me to the police station for further questioning,"

"No one has complained against me to be arrested and questioned."

"They will. I see butler is bringing the complaint." An old man approached them and the accused young man anxiously asked him whether the ladies have any complaint.

"No sir, not at all. In fact they invite you to come in." said the butler.

"Thank you, I can't. I have things to do."

"The lady is adamant that you are her grandson whom they

lost many years ago.

"But I have already told her, I am not her grandson."

"If you don't come in sir, I'm sure she will search the whole world to find you. To tell the truth, I have a feeling that she might be right." At this point young man turned to the racist policeman, who was listening to their conversation and said, "As you can see, this is a family matter and private conversation. No place for a stranger, may I ask you to leave?" He deliberately used the word of stranger to retaliate, which police did not like it and was about to respond when he saw the young lady coming towards them. "I have come to thank you for preventing injury to my grandmother," she said, "Please come in, she wishes to talk to you." Policeman had no choice but to leave them and young man remained undecided for some time. He was curious to find out more from the butler before accepting or rejecting the invitation.

"Thanks for the invitation but I have other matters to attend to. Please allow me to talk to my rescuer first, for a minute." He smiled and went on to say, "That police was just about to arrest me when this man arrived, with a message from your grandmother and saved me from a big trouble."

"I am sorry to hear that. Why did he want to arrest you?"

"He was suspicious of a stranger being here, looking inside the house. It is okay, I am not offended. But please don't wait for me; I'll join you if I can sort out the other matters with my rescuer's help." And after she left he asked the butler why he had a feeling that the old lady might be right.

"Well sir you remind me of the late husband of my lady. I mean your resemblance is what makes the lady to think that you're the boy who was stolen twenty eight years ago."

"Twenty eight years?" asked the young man startlingly, "How old was he at that time?"

"I think he was about four or five months, sir." This answer made the young man very sad and became silent for quite a long time. Butler noticed his concerns and preoccupation with something quite serious and decided not to break the silence.   The young man seemed struggling to control himself and put a worrying thought aside. Then, as if had come to a firm decision said, "Tell your lady that I am thirty one and therefore I cannot be her grandson."

"She will not believe me. I beg you to come in and say so yourself. It is hot weather here, you can have a bit of rest too; it is cool inside." Young man thought for a while and finally accepted the invitation mainly to eradicate his worrying thoughts by further enquiry. He then followed the butler while looking around, admiring the beautiful garden and remembering his childhood days once again. He saw the young lady anxiously standing in balcony, waiting to see whether he accepts the invitation or not. Clearly she was concerned about her grandmother and was not bothered about the young man at that time. She knew that if grandmother could not get more information from him it will be very difficult to console her. When the butler escorted the guest into a magnificent and luxuriantly decorated reception hall, he saw the old lady sitting in an armchair, eagerly waiting for the arrival of her assumed grandson, a middle-aged lady sitting next to her and a gentleman standing behind them, while the young lady was returning from the balcony who also remained standing. Apart from the butler there were also two female servants in the room; ready to receive instructions and orders.

CHAPTER 2

As soon as the young man entered the room, the middle aged lady jumped up with a joy and run towards him shouting; "My son, oh my dear son."   She was just about to cuddle and kiss the young man, when he managed to stop her by gently holding her shoulders with both hands and saying, "Please madam, control your-self.   I am not your son.   There has been a mistake."

"No, you are my son. You are exactly like your grandfather. There is no mistake. I can see it; I can feel it and I am sure you are..,." She then began crying loudly.   The gentleman behind the ladies came forward, looked at their guest with a strange mixture of affection and curiosity, then comforted his anxious wife with utmost care and love and sat her on her chair.

"I am awfully sorry that my accidental presence in this area has caused so much anguish to the ladies. I have heard from this man that you lost a few months old baby twenty eight years ago. Well, it cannot be me because I am thirty one years old, as simple as that."   He appeared very uncomfortable when he uttered these words. "Your birth certificate is forged one and wrongly shows you older." said the confident old lady, "We must investigate this."

"No madam," he answered, "it is a genuine certificate." But having said so, he became even more distressed and preoccupied. It was clear that he was not satisfied with his own declarations and answers. Something serious was bothering him.   He tried to control his emotion and to earn some time in order to return to his normal self, addressed the gentleman and jokingly said, "It is like a movie.   I left my noisy flat in search of a quiet place to think, then without realising I turned up in front of a house resembling my father's house, I made a lady faint then I was nearly arrested for attempted burglary in this private residential area and now; I am trying to convince these honourable ladies that I am not the person they think I am."

"In fact I am film producer," said the gentleman while smiling, "perhaps we could make a movie of this"

"The name of film should be resemblance," added the young man with a sad smile, "and I could help you in writing the scenario." This did not help and he remained very nervous. All present in the room noticed that he was not feeling well at all and therefore, kept their silence in expectation of another sentence that he seemed unwillingly trying to utter. Then suddenly he burst out, "Was the baby stolen in a village called Sarein?"

"Yes." shouted both ladies at the same time and synchronously asked, "How did you know that?"

"I have heard the story. It is a small place and the events such as this are not forgotten so easily." He now was flushing and sweating and appeared miles away.

"How did they tell the story?" asked the grandmother. He did not answer, as if had not heard the question but instead asked another question.

"Excuse me for asking this, but that place is a remote part of the country and even today hardly any foreign tourist goes there let alone so soon after the Second World War. Why did you go there at such a time? "

"It was my fault," said the old lady with a feeling of guilt evident on her face, "I never could forgive my-self. I wanted to find my husband's relatives, why at such a time I don't know. He was from a town near to that village and had told me about the amazing springs in Sarein; hot and cold mineral waters. We couldn't find his relatives and I thought now that we are there, I better try hot water for my joint pains. It was a tragedy; instead of finding the Azori family we lost our...," But she could not finish her sentence, as the young man stood up abruptly and shouted, "What? That is my mother's surname. Say no more. Don't say anything at all, not a single world please. I can't tolerate it any more. My head is bursting. I have been walking under hot sun for too long. I must pour cold water on my head." He was agitated, flushed and was sweating copiously. "Please forgive me I must do this. Show me the bathroom please." He said to one of female servants and as he was following her; repeated authoritatively while waving his finger in the air "No more, not a single word."

Everyone in the hall was extremely shocked and could not comprehend his emotional state which was shown from the moment that he arrived and now his final unexplainable behaviour and worrying look. In the bathroom he asked the girl to turn the cold shower on and pour on his head and then asked her for a towel and partially dried his head and face leaving the towel hanging round his neck. "I need fresh air," said he, "please take me to balcony." Following the servant he passed the reception, totally ignoring them and entered the balcony, which was beautifully furnished and pleasantly cool. He sat on a chair and held his head with both hands, resting elbows on a table before him. The young lady came to balcony carrying a jar of water and a glass. She put them on the table together with a box of Aspirin and said, "Your headache is from dehydration, you must drink plenty of water." She poured water into the glass and continued, "I am a doctor, trust me." The young man raised his head, looked at beautiful face of the doctor and drank two glasses of water one after the other. He checked the box, took two tablets out and swallowed them with more water.

"That is very good," said the young lady, while laughing, "You should always check what is offered to you by strangers." He looked at her face again and appeared sad. She sat beside him and held one of his hands but immediately withdrew and said, "Sorry." He looked back with a gloomy smile on his face. She could not understand the meaning of that sad smile and did not have time to ask either. Her father came out and said, "Are you alright young man?" "No," said the guest and then added, "But I will be alright.   I am awfully sorry for troubles I have caused. I must leave now. "You shouldn't," said the gentleman affectionately, "Rest for some time here we will give you a lift when you feel better."

"Thank you sir, but I need to call my mother before is late. It is almost night time, where she lives."

"You can call from here." said the young lady.

"Could I? But it is long distance call."

"Of course you can, it is no problem. We could use an extension and bring the telephone here if you prefer or you could use it in the hall."

"I will use it in the hall." They went in again and he sat on a chair beside the telephone and dialled and after a few seconds began talking with different language.   The middle-aged lady asked the old lady, "Mother, do you understand it?"

"Not quite but he is speaking Azeri with his mother."   By now another young man had come and was talking to young lady who was briefing him of the day's event.   They were siblings, the gentleman was their father, the middle-aged lady their mother, and old lady their maternal grandmother.   After few minutes their guest joined them clearly feeling a lot better.

"I profoundly apologise for my behaviour although I still beg you to maintain your silence until I report to you what my mother says."   The ladies keenly agreed and he began talking.

"My mother says; sometime between the two world wars her uncle left the native country and never came back. His name was Abdol-ali Azori."

"That is my husband," screamed the old lady and began weeping, "That is his name." she added. Young man stopped talking and looked at the lady with a mixture of compassion and surprise and then continued his report when the lady was calmer, having been consoled by her daughter.   "She says," said he, "he married with a Christian girl called Susan."   "That is me." said the old lady and began crying even lauder and had to be comforted once more, this time by her son in law and granddaughter. "He used to send letters and photos regularly," young man continued calmly," but no more since the Second World War."

"He was killed in the war." Said the son in law as the lady was still crying; unable to talk.

"My mother says," young man went on reporting, "the last photo he sent showed him with his wife and three children one of them a beautiful girl called Maryam."

"And that is my name. Oh God, this is unbelievable." uttered the mother of stolen baby and joined her mother to weep together; both astonished and bewildered. The young man, having finished the report, laughed like an insane but at the same time appeared relieved. The story which he was so concerned about was forgotten, at least for the time being. He managed to control his bizarre laughter and said; "It is all clear now." He then turned to the gentleman and continued, "Your film will have some turns and twists and rather difficult to believe. We need to change some parts to make it believable for the viewer." The ladies had stopped crying and were waiting to hear more as it seemed they had not yet digested the information.

"Can anyone believe it?" he laughed again facing the old lady, "Your late husband was my mother's uncle." Addressing the middle-aged lady continued, "Your father was my mother's uncle. You are my mother's cousin. I'm your cousin one removed." He laughed loudly, "Can anyone believe it? You went to find your husband's relative and twenty eight years later you found one of them standing behind the gate of your house fascinated by its architecture."

"Incredible," said the gentleman, "incredible indeed."

"And you were absolutely right about resemblance between me and your husband. It is the magic of genes madam. After all I am his niece's son, no wonder why I look like him."

"He was as handsome as you." said the lady tear in her eyes.

"He could not be as handsome as me," said the new relative and while laughing added, "it was a joke, sorry about it."

"Don't apologise, you are right," said grandmother, "but he would have been as handsome as you if he could get rid of his moustache. I kept asking him." They talked about this incredible coincidence for some time and all appeared quite relaxed now. In their conversation they found out that; he has been in this country for years, he is single and lives in a rented flat somewhere in London. But he did not tell them his name, education or occupation. "Just call me cousin please," he said, "and I work in a governmental institution." And after few minutes of further talks the new relative said to the middle-aged lady, "Madam, you keep looking at me, most likely remembering your father. Or perhaps you want to hug your cousin?"

"Yes please, yes." she said and run towards him, hugged and pressed him to her chest. She kissed, caressed his head, face and arms and even smelled him for some time and cried. The young man became rather uncomfortable and gently tried to separate himself from firm grasp of enthusiastic relative and light-heartedly said; "Madam, remember I'm cousin one removed and your husband is watching us." They all laughed and the lady, clearly embarrassed; said, "I am sorry. For a minute I felt I was cuddling my son. No, not just feeling, I was sure my son was in my arms." She began weeping again. Young man, tears in his eyes, took both of her hands and kissed. He then said, "I must go," and while smiling again added, "but before I do so I like to say hello to my cousins two removed." He then went towards the siblings who were sitting at the other side of the hall, and first said to the brother, "Cousin, if it was in my country, I would have hugged and kissed you but I know that it is not considered norm here so I just hug." He did so and asked, "What is your name and what is your profession?"

"My name is David and I am an engineer working in my father's company."

"So you help him in producing films." Then turning to sister jokingly said, "kissing ladies is not a problem here," he hugged and kissed her which she responded lovingly, "I know you are a doctor, which speciality you have chosen?" "Genetics,." answered the sister, which made their guest to turn to father and say, "Another coincidence sir. I mentioned wonders of gene and your daughter is a genetics expert. What should be the name of film; coincidence or resemblance?" He then continued talking to the young lady and asked, "What is your name?"

"Kathrine, what is yours and what you do?" There was a long delay in guest's answer but eventually he said, "No name or occupation for the time being as I am not sure whether I will come here again." The story that he had heard from his mother had returned to his conscious again and he did not wish to be traced and found; if he decided to put a premature end to this accidental acquaintance.

"What do you mean? You are our cousin and we would love to see you again."

"How do you know I am really your cousin?"

"You just proved it," said David, "why do you say such a thing?"

"What was the proof?"

"Your mother knew our grandfather's, grandmother's and mother's first names?"

"I could have asked their names from the butler before I came in and then pretend that my mother informed me over the telephone."

"You knew our grandparents have three children."

"I had enquired that too."

"How did you know the name of village that our brother was stolen?"

"I remembered from the story that my mother had told me. You see, it is likely that I used my information about the stolen boy, traced and found his wealthy family. Then I came here hoping to find an opportunity to execute my plan. My plan could be accidentally finding that my mother and yours are cousins in order to be part of the family and take advantage. So how could you be sure that I am not a criminal?"

"Obviously you are not criminal." said Kathrine rather crossed, "You are just teasing us. And what about the striking re-semblance between you and grandfather; how are you going to explain that?"

"Well, that was a pure chance." He laughed, "Anyway, I must go now." He went towards the seniors to say goodbye but they would not accept and insisted him to stay for dinner.

"We were all so captivated with the story that," said the father, "we completely forgot to offer you something to drink or eat. On Saturdays we usually have late lunch or early dinner and it is now almost three o'clock. Please stay for dinner."

"Many thanks, I have to prepare something for Monday, I better go. Please give me your card, I will call and come another day."

"Here is my card," he passed it to young man, "but we would like you to stay for dinner."

"In my opinion, you should move in and live in this house." said the grandmother, "This is your great uncle's house and you have a share in inheritance. He purposely built it big hoping to bring his older brother and his family to live in this country. He truly loved his brother."

"I don't know anything about the law regarding inheritance in this country but recently my father died and I formally disinherited myself from inheritance."

"Why did you do that?" asked grandmother but did not wait for answer. She talked about ambitions of her husband and how he would have been delighted, if he was still alive and could see his great nephew is living in the house that he partly built for that purpose. But the young man rather preferred to answer the question than listening to great uncle's ambitions.

"I can earn enough money to live comfortably and I thought my dear siblings could make good use of the inheritance." At this point he looked at the card and said, "Oh, you are that famous director. I've seen most of your films. I am honoured to have met you sir."

"You are very kind. Would it make more likely that you stay for dinner?"

"No, but I will certainly call and come to see you all."

"You didn't tell anything about the story you heard from your mother. Surely it must have been about our tragedy but I just wonder what people say about it."

"I'll ask details from my mother and tell you next time I am here. Perhaps it is not about you anyway." He then took his leave in spite of sincere insistence of his mother's cousin. She looked at him leaving the room and said inside "I can see he has become emotional again the same emotion that we saw earlier. I am sure there is something that bothers him and hides from us."

On the way to his place he was deep in thoughts. "Hopefully, story is not about what the ladies were talking about," he thought, "but what if the two tales are somehow related?" He prayed that it was not the case. He had just promised to visit that family again but now he was not so sure about it. "The less I know about this is the better." he said inside, "I must protect my mother that is the main thing." They had insisted the driver to take him home but he did not want him to learn the address, "Not yet anyway," he said inside and then, asked the driver to drop him in front of a hotel, "I'm going to meet someone here. Please don't wait for me and thank you for the lift." He went to the receptionist and pretended he is asking a question and once he was sure the driver had gone; went out of hotel, crossed the road and entered his apartment.

That night he hardly slept. The following day he called his mother again and told her the whole story. Mother was over the moon to hear the news and said, "I want to see my cousin, invite her and her family to come and see her father's native land." He didn't tell her that they had already been there with disastrous consequences. The story that he had heard from mother was a bit different but now he was worried that two stories might be the same. "No, that would be too much of a coincidence." he said inside, "These are separate events, I hope." He nearly asked his mother whether the day in which God gave a second life to her dead son, was there any foreign tourist at the same guest house, but he didn't. By no means; he would hurt his mother or bring doubt in her mind about the miracle son. He firmly decided to tolerate the distress of facing with the reality alone and not to disclose it to anyone else; if what he suspected proved to be correct.   He promised to mother that; either he will invite cousin's family as she suggests or bring her to UK to meet them.

CHAPTER 3

For few days he was uncertain what to do. On the one hand he very much wanted to find out the truth behind this unexpected encounter which led to discovery of a relation in UK and its relevance or connections to the story of miracle son. On the other hand, he did not want to cause disappointment, grieve and indeed devastations to his mother, whom he truly loved and worshiped. At the end he came to conclusion; "I will find out," he said to himself, "and suffer the consequences alone, if what I fear proved to be the reality. I'll not tell anyone at home and if I could, I will prevent any claim that my newly found relatives might have." He also felt obliged to help this family by ascertaining the truth and reassuring them that, the missing son is not dead and he is indeed alive and happy. But he did not want to rush in embarking on such a sensitive issue. Therefore, he decided to meet the family again but, decline telling that story, with the excuse that he needed more information from home before doing so. So, he made an appointment and went to his cousin's house at another weekend. They were indeed delighted to see him again. Interestingly, Kathrine appeared much happier than anyone else.

"I'm so glad to see you again," said the grandmother, "I cannot wait to hear your mother's version of the unfortunate story. Perhaps she can help us to find our son."

"Perhaps," said the young man compassionately, "but the story is not about your grandson. It is about another family, although I think there might be a link."

"Please tell what she said to you."

"Grandma," said Kathrine, "please don't rush. He has just arrived, let us offer something to eat and drink."

"Yes my dear, you are right. I will wait."

"Today, I only came to see you. I did not mean to tell the story. I am still waiting for some information from home and it will be wrong if I rush before clarifying certain points. Please be patient. If what I think turned out to be correct, probably we could trace your son. That is the only good news I can give you but please don't count on it too much; I might be wrong in assuming that there is a connection between the two stories."

"Cousin, it sounds rather mysterious," said the father, "but I trust you and we will all try to be patient. Let us talk about something else." After some usual hospitalities and general talks, young man said, "My mother is very anxious to see you and invites all of you to her house. I'm sure it could be a pleasant holiday and reunion. You will see a beautiful country, a different culture and meet tens of your cousins and hundreds of other relatives."

"Please thank her for the invitation," said the mother "I cannot wait to see my cousin. I am sure it will be a happy occasion to meet all of the relatives but she too could come here and stay with us for as long she wishes."

"Yes my dear." agreed the grandmother and turned to the guest and continued, "As I said the other day, your great uncle wished to bring his brother's family here. Now, we have the opportunity to fulfil his ambition. You and your mother should live here. I believe in soul and I know that, his soul will see both of you and will be very happy. The apartments that he built for this purpose have rarely been occupied by the guests. In fact one of the apartments was never used as far as I can remember." She then turned to the father and said, "Show him his apartment please."

"Thank you, I will pass your invitation and kind words to my mother."

"My husband loved her, we have a photo of her in family album and I will show you." One of the servants was sent for the album and as soon as it was brought, she started showing the photos one by one and the young man was astonished of the resemblance between himself and great uncle. When they got to his mother's photo from very young age; he recognised her and said, "That is my mother when she was only a girl."

"Yes," said the grandmother, "and my husband loved and longed to see her. I wonder if you have a recent photo of her."

"Yes I have," said he and reached to his pocket to show it in his wallet, "here it is."

"Oh what a beautiful lady she is." said the mother and Kathrine at the same time, "as a young girl, she was beautiful," added the mother, "but now she is even more beautiful; indeed stunning."

"I would love to put it beside the other photo," said the grandmother, "if you've another one like that."

"I can make a copy for you grandma," said David, "exactly like the original."

"Is it possible?" asked the young man.

"Yes, of course." They continued looking at the photo in album and soon the duplicate was ready to add in it, which grandmother did with care.

"Now that your photo demonstration is over my dear grandma," said the father eagerly, "it is my turn to show our guest, the apartment that you were talking about." He said so and directed the guest towards the separate apartments, which were connected through the corridors at either side of that reception hall. "The guest can lock the door if he prefers complete privacy," said the father, "or, leave it open for the servants, to clean the apartment every day. And of course, he or she can join the rest of the family through this door whenever wishes." He then showed three bedrooms with their on suite bathrooms, reception room, dining room, study room, kitchen etc. and added "There are television and radio in some of the rooms and separate telephone line too but the electricity, gas and water are connected to the main part of the house." Young man was very impressed with the details of construction, facilities and preparations for the expected guests.   His guide changed the subject to story of the designer of all these. "Soon after the First World War your great uncle migrated to this country. I'm told that he came with huge capital to start a business. He was an intelligent, highly educated and hard working person and to cut the long story short; well before the Second World War he became an extremely wealthy and influential man. In his position and at age he could avoid going to the war but he hated the fascism and loved his adopted country.   Therefore courageously went to the war and sadly just before the victory of allies, he was killed in action." While showing the residence he continued with the narration, "He is considered a war hero and has many medals in his name, which my mother in law keeps them as the most precious treasure.   But as he has left huge sum of money and other sources of income for his wife and children; she would not touch the government's pension for the war heroes and the money directly goes to the charity from her bank account." Once he had finished this brief history of the late owner of that magnificent house he said, "As you've heard from his widow, these separate apartments were meant to be your grandparents, your mother and indeed your own and your siblings' dwellings; if he had lived long enough and fulfilled his ambition of bringing his older brother and children to this country. It would be most appropriate if you moved in. You've not told us what is your occupation and it is not my business how much you earn but why should you pay rental when you have your own house here?"

"It is very generous offer sir.   This is a quiet lodging which is what I need and I am fed up with noise in my flat. So, I must think about it seriously but there are issues that I ought to consider. Thank you anyway."

"Think about it." said the father and went on showing the place, "Here is a door and steps behind it which takes you to the garden, with private parking area, garage and driveway. You will have remote control key for the gate and you can commute to the place of work or leisure without being disturbed by anyone."

"Oh my God, I must persuade myself to agree but honestly there are serious matters that I must consider before making any decision, sir."

"I leave it to you. Let us go for dinner." And they joined the rest of family. Over the meal there was only general conversation, without mentioning the extraordinary event in the recent days or questioning their guest. But after the dinner and while having tea and coffee; the old lady began encouraging him to move in and live with them. Mother joined the conversation and said, "My cousin will not forgive me if I don't look after her son here. Please move in as soon as you can and bring your mother to live with us too. You said that your father died and she is living on her own. It must be very lonely without your father and yourself." Young man promised to talk to his mother and arrange the trip, if she accepted the invitation. As for the moving in; he found it very attractive but did not promise to do so, wishing to think about the danger he was concerned about if imaginations turned out to be the reality. He had few minutes of chat with David and Kathrine and then took his leave from the seniors. He did not have a firm decision about new relatives' kind offer but at least in one matter he had made his mind; he was going to accept the eminent British professor's offer. "And what a wonderful place that apartment could be, for my study," he said to himself, "I wished they would accept the rental. But no, they will be offended if I suggest such a thing." And that was not the real issue to occupy his mind or bother him. He was worried about Kathrine and signs of affection that he had already seen on her face and behaviour. "It could turn out to be immoral and a serious issue," he said inside, "and in any case it is very unfair to her. Of course she will not understand even if I said this to her or anyone else. I have already decided not to tell anyone, at least not at this stage anyway. First, I need to stablish the facts and if I am right, how difficult it would be to make her understand without knowing the reason behind it. I am sorry for her but my mother is more important for me and I will protect her; whatever is the cost."

He had another sleepless night and from the following day, he decided to put the worrying things aside and keep himself busy with the preparation for training. Professor was delighted to learn that he had chosen his department rather than United States.

CHAPTER 4

Over the following few days; he talked to his mother about newly found relative's kind invitation and asked her advice regarding the appropriateness of him occupying one of their guest apartments in the house. Mother accepted their invitation with utmost delight, mainly to be with her son but also to see the cousin, which she had known about but never had dreamed to meet. She also advised her son to accept their offer as she was always concerned about him living on his own and was sure that her cousin would look after him like a mother.

"When you see them next," she said, "thank them for inviting me. But also suggest them to visit our country first, if they are free from their work and we could return together."

"I have already invited them but I will say it again." When he informed mother that he will remain in UK for the sub-speciality training she was very happy indeed; both because of the relatives that he could live with them or at least visit them often and also because she was sure that he will come home more often than he would if he was in USA. He began his training and more than ever desired to have a quieter and more comfortable lodging. So, he accepted their offer and moved into same apartment which was shown to him. This was of course contrary to his concerns for Kathrine and prayed that, his imaginations, suspicions and observations were all wrong. "I will be very careful anyway," he said to himself, "and I will arrange tests to prove one way or other."

Few weeks after he was settled in the new lodging and in the first opportunity; he requested to see the whole family for a serious matter. More than anyone else grandmother was eagerly waiting for such a meeting. At the request of her daughter and advice of son in law she had stopped pushing the young man for further revelation of the story which he had heard. But inside, she was counting the days to find out more about that story and its connections to their ill-fated saga. Once everyone was comfortably seating in the reception room and curiously waiting for the information which he was about to disclose; he first informed them of his first name, surname and the fact that he was a qualified surgeon, now training in the sub-speciality of neurosurgery. All of them were delighted to hear that he was indeed a doctor, Kathrine in particular. He then unsuccessfully tried to explain why he was reluctant to say all these earlier. "At this stage, I cannot tell you why I was reluctant to introduce myself," he said, "or why I was so indeterminate about accepting your kind offer of living in this excellent apartment for which I am very grateful. You will know the reasons sometime in future, I promise." He hesitated for a minute or so and then continued firmly, "First time that, I accidentally met you here and heard the sad story; I suddenly remembered another story which my mother had told me. This made me very concerned and uncomfortable. I am sure you all remember my emotional state at the time."

"Yes, you did not look well at all," said the grandmother, "and I was sure that, you knew more than what you admitted."

"Well, it was not directly about your story but I suspected a connection."

"Tell us, I can't wait anymore." said the old lady.

"I will tell you the story which has occupied my mind since I heard about your son. It is a very sensitive issue and it is only my wild imaginations that make the link a possibility." At this point father dismissed all the servants and young man went on with his narration, "About twenty eight years or so ago, a mother from a well-known and respectful family was feeding her few months old baby when he choked, stopped breathing and died in front of her eyes."

"So sad," said the mother, not yet knowing what it had got to do with their stolen son.

"She screamed with extreme horror, dropped on the floor and remained unconscious or, as the story says; she fainted. And when she came around her servant said, "All is well madam; your son is peacefully sleep in his cot." She then helped the lady to come forward and see for herself. She was over the moon and believed that it was a miracle and God had given a second life to her dead son. The servant reinforced that belief by pointing to the baby and saying, "Look madam, God's light has made him whiter and prettier now." Poor mother agreed while crying with utmost joy. Later on the story spread throughout the town and it was unanimously agreed that it was a miracle and there-after, the boy was called miracle son."

"Interesting story," said the father, "but I cannot see the link."

"The link comes with my wild imagination which I have not said yet." Everyone kept their silence, eager and anxious to hear more.

"With wicked and immoral part of my brain, I see the scene differently. I don't think that mother fainted. I think because of the action of defensive mechanism that we all have and acts when we face with unbearable pain, horror or tragedy; she actu-ally became wholly unconscious, for a much longer time than is expected from mere fainting. Dr Kathrine would kindly forgive my simplicity in describing the defensive mechanism. Well, I am only a surgeon." He smiled and turned to the father and jokingly added "Here comes the scene of a horrible crime in your film sir, we need few flush backs." But he instantly apolo-gised, "I beg your pardon, I should not try to be funny. Indeed it is a terrible crime if I'm correct in my hypothesis."

"I still don't get it," said the father, "but please carry on."

"This happened at a guest house in the village of Sarein, where other families were also staying in the nearby rooms." At this stage both mother and grandmother half raised from their seats with wide open eyes; trying to express their horror by saying something but could not utter a word and he continued, "One of the families could have been you. The servant would have seen your son who was exactly the same age as her lady's son. She could have realised that you were all out of the room, enquiring about the source of that terrible scream and she had plenty time in hand as the lady was still unconscious." He stopped for few seconds and said, "Sorry, I'm playing detective now, but I cannot help it. I've been thinking about this scene for days.   I see the servant uses wicked side of her brain and commits a terrible crime in order to please innocent lady who is unaware of the forthcoming dreadful sin and mischief.   She snatches your son, swaps their dresses, puts the living baby in the cot and hides the dead one, to get rid of later.   And all this is happening while you are desperately searching for your son and begging other guests to help.   Perhaps authorities are involved in searching which I very much doubt there was any in that village but I am sure, no one would have dared; to search that noble lady's room or even question her.   And of course she was totally unaware of what was going on outside because she was too absorbed in praying, meditating and thanking God for the miracle. I have no doubt that, the servant never told anyone what she did and so, that mother brought up your son genuinely and innocently believing he is her own." They were all dead silent and could not believe or even understand what they were hearing, until the most familiar one with strange stories amongst them woke up and managed to control himself.

"Fascinating imagination." said the father.

"You are right, that must be what happened," said the grandmother having recovered from initial shock and horror "we went out to see what the problem was and when we came back to the room, our beautiful baby was not in his cot."

"We searched everywhere that we could think of," said the mother with broken voice" and after hours of waiting, a gendarme arrived but, he did nothing except for looking at the places that we already had looked."

"I am not surprised. Even today there is hardly any police (let alone detective) in that part of the country to investigate such matters."

"When we eventually managed to inform our embassy, and asked for help, they couldn't do anything about it either." said the mother while crying pitifully, "And we had to return home with broken hearts and guilty feeling; why did we take a baby to such a strange place."

"I am sorry; it seems that I have refreshed the agony and grief you felt at the time. But the reason behind such a painful recall is that if I am right, there is a hope that I could help you."

"Do you know that family?" asked father excitedly.

"Everyone knows that family." He answered.

"Please help," pleaded the mother and grandmother together.

"I do not want to create too much hope for you.   Please bear in mind that, it is only a theory and merely an imagination, I might be absolutely wrong."

"It is a possibility," said the father, "could you trace them? I mean does your mother know where they might be now?"

"I am sure she knows but we must be very careful. I have not asked her yet and when I do, by no means will I tell her what I have just described to you."

"Why?" asked father.

"For various reasons but I can't go through at this stage. I can only say that accusing such family, particularly if it turns out to be false, could have serious consequences. Moreover, any investigation could be impossible. I mean if anyone else, including my mother, hears this; we cannot stop the spread of our suspicion and that family, will definitely refuse any cooperation in investigation."

"Do as you see right please," said grandmother, bring our son to us." She began crying.

"The only thing I promise is to prove that he is alive and happy. You've lost all hopes over these long years and perhaps you have assumed that he was kidnapped and murdered. It will be wonderful news if you find out that he is alive. Am I right in saying so?"

"Yes," said the father, "but if your hypothesis proved to be correct and you found him, it is our right, legally and morally, to have him back to where he should have been, if not stolen."

"It is not as simple as that," said the young man evidently preoccupied with his thoughts.

"What do you mean?"

"I will help you to find out that he is alive and happy but not to take him from his mother."

"What?" shouted father.

"But my dear cousin, I am his mother.   Shouldn't I have my son back after mourning for more than twenty eight years and longing to find him?"

"His mother is as sure as you are that, she is his mother. We cannot destroy her life."

"Mother," entered Kathrine in conversation for the first time, "cousin has a point there, we must think what should be done without causing any serious harm to someone else."

"We haven't yet proved anything," said the young man, "and it sounds rather premature to talk about such a subject.   But now that the point has been raised; I ought to clarify what I mean, before going ahead with the investigation."

"I agree that we do not know yet whether your hypothesis is just an imagination or not," said the father having calmed down, "or will turn out to be a reality. But I am interested to hear; what is your objection to our legal and moral rights?"

"Most likely; that mother has loved and cared for her son for more than twenty eight years.   How could you justify taking her son away from her?"

"How did they justify stealing our son in the first place?"

"She must be absolutely unaware of that crime."

"It seems you personally know this woman," said the father rather harshly, "and that's why you are defending her."

"She is a lady" said the young man clearly upset about the language that father used, "but I do not only defend her. I am defending all mothers including my cousin here." He then turned to mother and continued, "How would you feel if someone comes in and proves that, David is not your son and take him away from you? How David will feel if he was taken to another country, shown entirely strange people and be told that; these are your parents and relatives? Will you not feel devastated; for losing a son whom you've loved and cared as your own son since he was a baby? How will David find himself in a strange country, where he probably doesn't speak their language and does not know anything about their culture? Could you for a minute put yourself in place of that lady and her son? Don't get me wrong, I understand your feelings and am aware of your rights but I cannot accept destroying that lady's life nor put her son in a difficult position. We must act sensibly and cautiously. I'm as keen as you are; to find the truth, please believe me." He tried hard to show his impartiality but virtually everyone present in the room, could see and feel his profound respect and care for the lady in question. And there was a truth in that feeling. However after that long speech, there was a silence and then mother said, "But that is what happens in the adoption. Children want to trace their biological parents when they are adults. I'm sure my son would want to do so."

"Adoption is a different matter," responded the young man, "in such cases; parents already know that they are not biological parents. And most of the times, as the child get older; they gradually let him or her know the truth. Of course you are right some of these children wish to find their biological parents but, you appreciate that there is a big difference here."

"We see the difference," said the father, rather frustrated, "let us hear how you're going to help us anyway?"

"As soon as I can secure leave from my training and work, I will go home. I hope I will be able to find him and bring a sample of blood for genetic analysis.Dr Kathrine will instruct me in which tube I should use and in what condition I should provide the sample. I can pretend that it is for research and of course I will not put his real name on the tube."

"Why?" asked the father.

"That is to protect the mother and child."

"Once the sample is available," said Kathrine, "I will take samples of blood from Mum and Dad and let you know if they genetically match; it is getting very exciting. Is it possible to find our older brother? It seems like a dream to me."

"I am sure we will find." said grandmother confidently.

"Could that sample match with one but not with the other?" asked David, with laugher and then immediately added, "Sorry that meant to be a joke."

"Well," said the father trying to show that he is not frustrated or angry with the young man, "it could open another line of enquiry in the film."

"I pray you will soon go to your country and find our son." said grandmother, "And please bring your mother with you. We all wish to see her. My husband was so fond of his niece and longed to see her."   They talked for hours about the possibilities, their hopes and difficulties that may arise. The young man did not participate in the talks as much as was expected; at times he seemed miles away. He was thinking about his mother but also about Kathrine who had expressed too much love and care for him and that was precisely what he feared could happen, if he moved in and practically lived with them. Since he had occupied that apartment, Kathrine often came to see and talk to him.   Sometimes it was about the medical subjects or social matters but often she would express her love to him either by spoken words or body language. Once she looked at his pretty face for some time and said, "I love you."

"I love you too," answered the young man, "I love all of you; we are relatives."

"I mean, I have fallen in love with you." said Kathrine and blushed.

"Don't, that is morally wrong."

"What do you mean? We are cousins two removed; we are not that close relatives."

"There are reasons that I cannot tell you now."

"Are you married? Is that why you say; it is morally wrong?"

"I am not married, but it is something like that."

"You are engaged then. You love someone else."

"That is not the case either."

"Or you don't find me attractive enough."

"You are the most beautiful girl that I have seen and I love you like my sister.One day I will tell you the reason but for now let us love each other like siblings." She was upset and cried but did not stop coming and seeing him hoping he too will fall in love. The young man treated her like a sister all the time. It was a couple of weeks later that he arranged to meet the family as described earlier. He thought the truth must be known at least to him, before is late but by no means he would cause any harm to his mother. He managed to take leave and went to bring his mother to United Kingdom. And when he was saying goodbye to the family once again he asked not to talk about it with anyone including his mother.

"She does not speak English of course but in any case please make no mention of your son that was stolen or the family that I am about to investigate." He explained further and having obtained their promise he embarked on his errand.

CHAPTER 5

Less than two weeks later, young man returned, happily escorting his mother. There was an emotional reunion between the two cousins with mixture of tears, laughter and joy. Everyone else in the family was delighted to meet their new relative, in particular the grandmother; who hugged and kissed her several times and said, "Welcome home my dear. I kiss you on behalf of your uncle too who sadly did not live long enough to witness that his dreams and hopes are fulfilled." The son began his duty as an interpreter and through him, the guest responded to their warm and kind welcome, with due courtesy and love. The old lady almost immediately sent one of the servants to bring her photo albums. She wished to show their guest her uncle's photos and that of her own, when she was only a young girl. A big banquet had been prepared to mark the arrival of their honoured guest and they all enjoyed that special occasion. From the following day, they began showing her different parts of London and country. Most of the times mother would escort her cousin but sometime father or David would join them too. And very occasionally one of the doctors would find spare time to show her around or join the two mothers in their walks and sightseeing etc.

Of course, young man had passed the sample of blood to Kathrine on arrival but had asked her to let him know the result first and not to tell it to parents immediately. "If the result was positive," he had said, "We should let them know when my mother is not there. By no means should she hear the story or the result of such test." Kathrine had agreed to do so but, could not understand his extreme cautiousness in this matter, even though, she had accepted that the life of the lady in question should not be ruined. "But why is he hiding it from his own mother?" she had wondered, "Would she tell anyone if she knows?" The result of genetic analysis was positive and Kathrine, with utmost delight, informed her cousin as promised. Then, together they arranged a meeting with the rest of family to announce the wonderful news to them but of course while his mother was resting in her apartment. There was indescribable ecstasy and interest shown when they heard the good news. There were shouting of the happiness, crying of the extreme joy and endless bombardment of questioning and seeking the reassurances.

"I can't believe," said father, "Could it be true? Have we really found our son? Is that true dear cousin? You have found him; I love you."

"I knew we will find," said grandmother while crying, "I can't wait to see him." And the mother kept crying with joy, hugging her cousin, every few minutes, kissing him and asking, "Is it true?" and turning to her daughter and asking "Kathrine; does the test say he is our son? I can't believe it." It seemed they could not stop repeating these words, could not stop crying with joy and could not even sit in one place. Of course the young man could understand their reactions and emotional state. They had waited for more than twenty eight years for such news and so, he calmly answered their recurring questions. And when they insisted on seeing the son, unlike the previous occasions, he did not rule out that possibility. They promised not to tell anything to his mother and went on thanking him again and again and hardly anyone slept that night.

*

However the honoured guest had a lovely time for few months, although, there were some ups and downs in her general well-being. One day she said to her son, "Take me back home, I have taken too much of their time."

"They love you to stay longer, I know it for sure but I will do as you wish.   Except that I've arranged a full check-up for you and once it was done we can go."

"There is nothing wrong with me, why check-up?"

"You have complained of tummy ache on and off and have also lost weight recently."

"That is because of exercise here. I never walked this much at home."

"We will do the check-up anyway; it is necessary. I am a doctor mother, remember?"

"Okay, how long will it take?

"It won't be more than a couple of weeks."   And the tests were carried out with shocking results. Son was devastated; his mother had pancreatic cancer.   It was rather advanced and he was aware of poor prognosis. After receiving all the results and talking to various specialists he cried in his office for long time before coming home. He first talked to Kathrine about the bad news and asked her not to tell anyone yet until he talks to his mother first and he did so. The following morning he did not go to hospital and after breakfast talked to his mother in her apartment. He tried very hard to present himself calm and not too worried.   When mother was informed of the results she said, "I will see the doctors at home. Now that the check-up is over; book the flights."

"No mother, treatment is better to be in this country. We don't have this level of speciality and expertise at home."

"What is the treatment that we don't have at home?" And son had to gradually say more about her condition and the fact that, the treatment might be a combination of different things such as surgery, medicine and perhaps radiotherapy.

"How long will the treatment take?" asked mother who now seemed very upset and fearful; having realised the seriousness of her condition.

"We will go together and the doctors will explain everything to you."

"You are a doctor, tell me yourself."

"I am not in that speciality but I think it will take weeks if not months."

"No I can't stay here that long, take me home please." And when son with all sorrows of the world in his heart and mind, explained why such a long and specialised treatment must be done in that country she said, "Take me home. I want to die in our own country and buried beside your father."

"Don't say that mother," said the son tear in his eyes, "everything will be fine. Nowadays they can treat such disease successfully. We will go back when you have recovered." But she insisted to return home. Young man thought that, he needs help to convince the patient and therefore, asked her permission to inform the hosts of the situation and she did not mind. Over the rest of that day first her cousin and later on Kathrine talked to her and finally she agreed to see the doctors and decide later. She had learned English enough to understand simple sentences but still needed translation in serious conversations.

In meeting with specialists, they managed to persuade the patient to forget about returning home for the time being and instead; agree to be admitted to the hospital as soon as possible to be prepared for the surgery and the chemotherapy. Because of the size and location of the tumour surgery was not as successful as they desired and therefore, not only the chemotherapy had to be intensified but later on radiotherapy was required too. For weeks and months she suffered of side effects of the chemotherapy, cycle after the cycle, from side effects of radiation and from local or systemic infections but never complained. In spite of losing her hair, weight loss to the extent of emaciation and indeed cachexia; she still looked beautiful and dignified. Son had numerous sorrowful days and nights, hours of crying and praying in his loneliness of office or apartment and in spite of being a doctor and knowing poor prognosis refused to lose hope. The whole family shared in his worries but Kathrine more than anyone else. She visited his mother regularly in hospital and the son, often in his apartment. Once the doctors lost all hopes and there were nothing else to offer, they talked to him and suggested to transfer his mother to a hospice for the terminal care. But the family strongly rejected such an idea and with all care and love brought her home. Specially trained nurses for terminally ill patients were employed and she was looked after at home, by a skilful team and with highest care and affection of her son and all members of the family. A few days later she desired to talk to her son privately.

"You don't need to hide anything from me. I know that I am dying. I had excellent life and have lived long enough. It is now prime time to return to God and be with my husband again. I ask you not to grieve too much," her son had begun crying, "I want you to be strong. I'm so glad to find my cousin and be with you these past months." She had talked for longer time than her condition allowed and therefore rested for a minute while her son putting his head on her hand and kissing it; continued crying.

"I have a request and I will be very upset if you refuse. Take me home; I want to die in our own country."

"But mother," he raised his head, "You are too weak to travel."

"I am sure you can arrange it. I've enough money and my cousin's husband has influence in this country. Do it before it is too late." After the last sentence, she closed her eyes and fell sleep.

A private jet was hired. Special arrangements for the rules and regulation of airport in leaving the country were made and the nurses attended the patient throughout the flight. Son, cousin and Kathrine were in the flight too. At the other end his brothers were waiting and an ambulance had been allowed to be brought beside the aircraft after the landing. There was no major problem in transferring the patient to her magnificent house where all of their close relatives were waiting to see her and, servants (with tear in their eyes), were anxious to receive their lady. It didn't take long; only three days later she passed away peacefully. Everyone was grieved of course but the young man was inconsolable and siblings, cousin and Kathrine had to work really hard to calm him down. Grandmother, her son in law and David came for the funeral. They stayed only for few days afterwards but the young man decided to stay a bit longer. The day before their departure, cousin cautiously and with profound apology said to him, "Is there a possibility of seeing our son before we go?"

"I will show him to you in England, I promise."

"Thank you," said the cousin, "and sorry for asking it at such a sad time."

"Don't apologise please, I know how much you long to see him. But he is not in a good state of mind at the moment and I better organise something when I join you."

"Is he okay? I worry when you say he is not in good state of mind."

"He is okay, don't worry." And they flew back to United Kingdom; heartbroken because of loss of the lady but at the same time, joyful and hopeful that they would soon see their son, when the cousin joins them and he did so after a week.

Before returning to adopted country he spent some time with his siblings and close relatives to settle certain legal matters and arranged his further visits to native land. During his mother's sickness and after her death he had taken too much annual or compassionate leaves and so he was anxious to return to his training as soon as possible After returning to United Kingdom for few weeks, emotionally he was not in a state of mind to execute his promise to the cousin but eventually persuaded himself to do what was so essential for that family and he had neglected for too long to protect his mother from any harm. When he had recaptured his training and work, once again he asked to see the whole family together. Hopeful mother anticipated that young man wants to arrange their meeting with their son as had promised, but when he asked for their permission, to see Kathrine separately in his apartment before talking to them, she got a different idea and whispered to grandmother.

In his apartment, when unaware Kathrine heard what her, so called cousin, wanted to tell her before meeting the rest of family; she screamed with utmost agony, wept and repeatedly punched on his chest and then hugged him and kissed but again began punching him. "Why didn't you tell me this before?" she said, "but it is not true, you are lying. You are teasing me." Then she said, sorry and put her head on his shoulder and started crying again pitifully.

"How could I lie to the most beautiful girl that I have ever seen in my life?   I am not lying, it is true.   You know why I couldn't tell you before.   I had to be very cautious; how could I allow my mother, that wonderful lady to grieve."

"I know."

"I want you to come with me and help mother when I inform them all. I am sure she will need you."   He kissed her forehead and both her hands and hugged her. "Let us join them now," he added, "they are anxiously waiting."   And they walked towards the main reception where everyone was seating and butler and servants were there too.

CHAPTER 6

Before they re-joined the rest of the family, who were waiting in the reception room; it was all nervousness but no talking until the proud mother leaned towards the grandmother and whispered again, "I'm pretty sure that he is going to propose. I know they are in love."

"That would be nice," said grandmother, "she cannot find any better."

"To tell the truth, Kathrine is in love with him but so far he has treated her as his sister."

"I don't blame her; I too fell in love with your father and proposed to him to marry me."

"You hadn't told me that before." said mother and they laughed. After few more minutes Kathrine and the young man came in and sat very close to mother. Again, father dismissed the servants as he was expecting private talks but, the young man said to the butler, "You stay please we may need you. And take a seat it might be a long talk." Butler sat on a seat near the door.

"First of all I must apologise," said the young man respectfully, "for lying to you, hiding certain things and being economical in truth." They waited to hear more. What lies? They asked inside.

"When I first saw you, I lied about my age. You were so excited and emotional with the likeness that you had noticed between me," here he turned to grandmother and went on, "and your husband madam, that I had to calm you down by a little lie. And I was not so sure about the relevance of story that I had heard from my mother and your sad story. At that encounter I was precisely twenty eight years and five months not thirty one that I said." The eyes of mother and grandmother were wide open. They were expecting to hear something about the proposal and even now they thought that, he was just trying to make himself perfectly known to them before asking their permission to marry Kathrine. Young man paused for a short time and continued; clearly trying hard to talk as calmly as possible. "Of course the accidental finding of our relativeness made sense for such a resemblance, between me and my mother's uncle. And therefore, I accepted the genes' work; as the explanation for that likeness except that it was too much for that sort of relationship. At the same time I could not ignore the story that I had heard from my mother, nor I could justify doing nothing to help you." All present in the hall were listening carefully but did not know where his narration was going to take them. He made another pause and now rather nervously, got to the serious part of his talk. "Many times you heard me telling that I did not want to cause any distress and grief to that lady by proving my hypothesis. I would not have forgiven myself, if I were the cause of pain, disappointment and bereavement to any mother, let alone to that honourable lady. Therefore my condition for assisting you to find your stolen son was that by no means should anyone outside this family know the reality and you must not take any legal action to claim your son. I do hope you appreciated why I insisted on that point."

"We fully understood," said the father, "why our actions should not cause any serious harm to that mother, who innocently had assumed he is her son for almost three decades. But you too appreciate that now that we know he is our son, we desperately want to see him." Mother and grandmother, with tears in their eyes, repeated that desire.

"I agree with what you say sir, and I must say that, the situation has changed a great deal now. Your son knows that you are his biological parents and sadly his mother has passed away."

"It is a awful thing what I am about to say;" said the mother, "and I'm really ashamed of myself but I cannot hide that, I am glad to hear the situation has changed and we can now see our son." Father tried to help his wife by saying, "One is never happy to hear that a person has died no matter how stranger he or she might be but sometimes a sad occasion such as this one may solve a moral issue."

"Indeed, the lady of that story was my mother." Everyone except for the Kathrine, almost synchronously, leaned forward with wide eyes and open mouths as if shouting, "What are you saying?" He did not want to stop. It was difficult task but had to be done. "The blood sample I gave to Kathrine was mine." Father and mother jumped up on their feet not quite knowing what to do or say. Their faces turned very pale and sweaty and it seemed they were totally unable to do or say anything. They looked completely paralysed except that they were both shaking uncontrollably. Young man stood up too and signed to Kathrine about the upcoming reaction which will need her assistance and went on with what he had started, and knew that, there was no turning back. "The miracle son of that story was me. Father, mother I am your son." Mother screamed hysterically and continually, rushed towards him, hugged him with shaking arms, kissed him but could not stand on her feet and fell down. Kathrine reached her immediately, cuddled and began reviving and calming her. Butler brought a glass of water and mother managed to have a sip. Meanwhile the father came towards the young man and faintly managed to say, "Is that true?"

"Yes father, I am your son." He hugged him, kissed and began crying very load. Butler had never seen his boss crying; he too began crying. David was fixed in his seat with tears in his eyes, grandmother was crying silently and in between the sobs was saying the things that, nobody heard or understood, and father had put his head on his son's shoulder; still sobbing. Mother recovered but not enough to raise herself up and so crawled slowly and hugged her son's feet. Kathrine separated mother and while herself overwhelmed with that scene and crying, tried to calm her.   Son kissed his father and gently led him to his seat and retuned to mother. He lifted her up like a baby and placed her too on her seat and said, "Calm down mother. Don't cry and do not try to talk either. Just take big breathe and relax."

"Come to me my boy," said grandmother, "I can't get up." He went to the old lady and she pressed him to her chest, kissed and said, "I knew you are my grandson even after finding out that lady is my husband's niece.   Not that I could have imagined of what you've told us but I just could not forget my first instinct. God bless that wonderful lady." and she began sobbing again. Miracle son went towards David and said, "I can now kiss you my brother."   He then hugged and kissed him three times and jokingly added, "Three times is routine in my country, and some of other countries such as France."

"I still can't believe," said David, "do I have an older brother?"

"Yes you do David."   David hugged his brother and would not let him go.   They gradually relaxed and believed the strange and unexpected reality. Mother and grandmother stopped crying and began thanking God. Mother still ashamed of being happy to hear that the lady of story, her own cousin, died so she put her hand on her face and said: "Please forgive me for saying that, I was glad to hear the change in situation. I know how much you loved that wonderful lady, my beautiful cousin. I loved her too. How sad it is that, she died so unexpectedly."   And again began crying and son hugged and kissed her hand. Thereafter from time to time, mother got up and kissed him again.

"Don't spoil me mother," said he, "my Azeri mother has already spoiled me enough."   Tear filled his eyes and with a broken voice continued; "She was a wonderful mother, a truly noble and most remarkable lady and a role model in society."

"Yes my dear, she was," said mother, "and exceptionally beautiful too. I loved her and will always remember her. God bless her soul." At this moment butler said, "I know it is not my place to talk but please allow me to say something. She was indeed a lady from upper class. She walked, talked and behaved like a queen. I was honoured to have been at her service. I served a queen; I will treasure that honour for ever. God bless her soul and that of her uncle." It was not norm for butler to enter in conversation but that was an extraordinary situation and in fact his remarks touched all of them.   They celebrated the occasion with champagne and things to eat which were provided hastily by butler and servants.   Afterwards once again they sat down to talk about their dreams that had come true.

"I would like to clarify fa ew points if I may," said the miracle son, "I have lied to you in the past, I could lie again about being your son."

"Don't start again." shouted Kathrine, "you said the same when you were our cousin."

"And I was right; I am not your cousin." They all laughed and Kathrine agreed with smile."But seriously," he continued, "it could come into mind of people that I saw the opportunity to change my status from a cousin to a son, now that I have had enough time to see how much wealth is in the family."

"No one will say that," said father, "We've no doubt that you are our son. We could see it right from the day one, but as you have said, this relationship and wonders of genes made us to accept another reality."

"But in any case, to make sure that at least no stranger would think otherwise," son continued, "I have asked my solicitor to produce this document in which I've disinherited myself from my grandfather's, grandmother's and parents' inheritance. Of course, all the names have come in their proper places in the document."

"Very silly thing to do." said the old lady, "You did the same silly thing after dear cousin's husband died. I remember you saying."

"There was no need at all for such a thing my son." said father and mother repeated it.

"David; please," said son while handing the document to

David, "keep it in safe place."

"There is no reason for it." answered David.

"In the land that I was brought up, hierarchy within the family is strictly observed. When the older asks or orders something, the younger one obeys."

"In that case I will keep it but we will not need it." Grandmother asked David to throw the document away; saying that she could feel her husband's soul is distressed with what he sees.

"The other thing that I want to be done is repeating the blood test." said the older brother, "I want Kathrine to take blood from me, Mom and Dad and repeat the genetic analysis."

"Is that an order sir?" said Kathrine while laughing.

"Yes it is." said he while smiling and then added, "It is a request."

"Okay, I will do but I don't need blood from Mom and Dad. We still have the remaining of sample that you gave me; all I need to do is to see your blood matching with it."

"These are all unnecessary things," said mother, "but thank you for sparing us. I don't like needles."

"I would be happier if full genetic analysis was done. But I am not expert in this filed; do what is right and please do it very carefully."

"Sure, you know that I've an interest here to prove you wrong." Having said this, Kathrine blushed and then added, "Mom knows and I better confess to others too." She had a sad smile on her face, "I fell in love with my cousin but thank God he already knew I am his sister."

"I don't blame you." said grandmother, "I fell in love with your grandfather at first sight. I remember very well."

"Tell the story please." said mother, to help Kathrine as she seemed rather uncomfortable after the confession. Grandmother looked around to see if they were alone in the room and mother reassured her that the servants and butler had gone to get the dinner ready. So, she started her story.

"I was going into a shop when a young man who was coming out of it, accidentally blocked my way in. He apologised with his beautiful foreign accent and passed.　　He was very handsome, smartly dressed gentleman, well behaved and well spoken. I fell in love there and then and could not let him go. I mean I could not miss my chance. So I turned back and followed him."

"Naughty girl." said Kathrine and laughed; she seemed back to her normal self now.

"I was not naughty; I just fell in love." said the grandmother smiling, "I found out that he was a businessman.　I learned his name, the address for his office and then with the help of one of my friends met him several times in different occasions.　Poor man had no idea that all those supposedly accidental meetings were planned by my friend. The handsome man always treated me with respect but, never said anything to show that he wanted to see me more often.　I was disappointed and very upset, as I was a young and pretty girl and had done all I could to attract his attention without getting anywhere."

"I am sure he was just busy with his business." interrupted mother.

"May be but I was fed up. At the end of a party I pushed him into a corner and said, what's wrong with you Mr Azori? He said he did not know what was wrong with him.　I said; don't you see that I am in love with you? He said, sorry I have not noticed.　I got really angry with him, kissed him and said, now that you know; will you marry me? He smiled and said, he would think about it. Anyway, a few months later we married."

"So you forced grandfather to marry you." said Kathrine.

"I did not force him; he too fell in love with me, without any further effort from my side."　They all laughed.　Dinner was ready and therefore Kathrine could not ask about the details. They enjoyed the special dinner very much, now that the whole family were together. After the dinner they sat around for drink and more talks. Ladies had tea and coffee and the gentlemen continued with the wine that had started over the dinner. Father drank excessively, David moderately and his older brother very little. Grandmother kept saying she wished her husband was alive to see his grandchildren and his niece. "None of his grand children were born," she said, "when he was killed in the war." Tears came to her eyes and miracle son hugged and kissed her to console and tried to bring her thoughts to something else.

"I have not seen my uncles yet," said he, "where are they?"

"My dear brothers are too busy running father's empire which is scattered both sides of the Atlantic." said the mother, "One of them is always in United States and the other, all over the places in Europe. We hardly see them."

"They kept calling and asking about dear cousin when she was in hospital," said the father, "even suggested to transfer her to States if you felt they have better facilities over there."

"Yes they did" said the son, "I'm very grateful. They also sent beautiful bunches of flower almost every week with well-wishing cards. It was indeed very kind of them."

"I think they should reduce the size of business," said father, "and at least think about their own families if not us, and spend more time with them."

"In fact, according to the Financial Times they are increasing the size." said David, "As major shareholders; perhaps we should persuade them to stop making more money and think of the family life more than what they do now and of course think of their own health too."

"That is true." said grandmother, "What is the point of making more money, if they don't have time for their wives and children."

"Where do they live?" asked the miracle son, "I mean their family."

"One in United States and the other in Germany." she answered, "We sometimes go and see them. They have not been here for years."

"I'm going to bed," said the father clearly very tired and sleepy, "from tomorrow morning; we will continue celebrating all the weekend. I hope doctors are not on call for the weekend." Neither miracle son no Kathrine were on call. Butler

was ordered to prepare big banquets for two days. Shortly afterwards grandma and mother retired too and the younger ones
continued chatting for some time having sent butler and servants to rest too as they had to wake up early in the morning to
prepare the banquets.

"I find it difficult to believe that we have found our brother,"
said Kathrine; while hugging and kissing older brother, "It
seems to me that I am dreaming."

"There is no proof yet that, I am your brother," said her
brother teasingly, "you should wait for the result of the test."

"Don't start again," said the sister angrily, "I am going to bed,
good night."

CHAPTER 7

They resumed their celebration from the late Saturday morning which continued the entire weekend as father had wished.   Following the dinner on Saturday night and after an hour or so chatting during which the older brother had hardly said anything, and appeared completely absorbed in his thoughts; he suddenly began talking.

"I loved my Azeri mother very much and I would have rather died than seeing her grieved by this revelation. I will always remember her and treasure excellent memories that I have from that perfect human being. It is indeed a pity that she didn't speak English for you to appreciate her qualities." Here, mother interrupted and said that she had picked up quite a bit of English but, miracle son didn't think that it was sufficient for what he meant and continued to praise , "She was highly educated lady, well read and extremely intelligent and had an extensive comprehension of social, moral and spiritual aspects of the life. When she talked about such matters seriously; one would think that she must be a great philosopher and in a way she really was."

"Even though that much-loved lady didn't speak English fluently," said the father, "but I must say that I was very impressed with her amazing qualities. God bless her soul.   She suffered a great deal with her illness and I admired her for the fact that she didn't change.   She remained the same honourable lady, the same adorable person.   My dear son, I can see why you loved her so much. Your love is not merely because she was your mother since you were a baby but also because she was such an extraordinary noble human being." Tears fell from son's eyes.

"She never complained either." said Kathrine, "I have never seen a patient; as tolerant as she was." They remembered her sufferings as well as her strong character and dignity. Sadness filled their hearts and for some time they forgot about the celebration.

"You were absolutely right," said grandmother, "not to let her know the reality. I could not forgive us if we were the cause of grief for her. I say this not because she was my husband's niece, my daughter's cousin or your Azeri mother, as you call her, but because she was such a wonderful lady; an innocent and honest person. She suffered a lot of course but, at least it was for another unfortunate reason not because of our selfishness."

"That is perfectly true." said mother, "In fact I admire you for protecting such a delightful lady. Truly I myself fell in love with her and I am so sad that she passed away at that age."

"She was only sixty," said the son with a broken voice, "not considered old nowadays".

"True," said father "but life goes on my son. I am sure if she could speak to you now, she would advise you; stop mourning and enjoy the life, which she cherished, cared and protected for you." He then gradually managed to change the subject and once again they began enjoying the wine, tea or coffee and of course talking. The topics of conversation were either related to their utmost delight of finding their son or their sincere grief of losing dear member of the family.

"There have been numerous children who were kidnaped, abused and even murdered or at times were raised by another family but this is indeed incredible." said the miracle son, "But who could believe that your son was stolen by a wicked person and then cared, loved and brought up by your own cousin whom you had never seen before? And who could believe that twenty eight years later that son intuitively turned up behind the gate of his biological parents' house and immediately was recognised by his observant grandmother?

"It is really incredible," agreed the father, "It is a miracle from the start to end."

"You may need to make some changes in the scenario of the film," said the miracle son jokingly, "otherwise   no one will believe the story."

"Well, although this story is fascinating but for a film it is too short." said the director," So, it will be helpful if we accept David's joke I mean if the father's blood did not match; not only it would open another line of enquiry and exploration but also it would prolong the story and therefore the film."   He then turned to his wife and said, "I apologise darling, we are talking about the film just for fun."

"People like that sort of things and easily accept it as a norm nowadays," said David, "and it could persuade them to believe the rest of the story too."

"Very sad," said grandmother, "if that is true."   They continued talking about producing a film out of their story but more jokingly than seriously. From here on although miracle son was participating in the conversation but actually his mind was somewhere else again. By this time he had lived in that country for more than thirteen years. But he was not yet feeling at home and the people there seemed to him like strangers than his own people.   One could accept it as a natural, or at least expected feeling, because he was brought up in another country and entirely different culture. He had many tender memories from his childhood time; from the care, protection and love which he had received from his childhood parents or from his friends and relatives.   He really loved that country and her natural beauty, her people, its history and their culture.   In particular he admired the music of that nation. "How could I forget them?" he said inside, "How could I ignore my debts to those kind people who brought me up and helped me to achieve my potentials and get where I am now?"   He felt himself in a difficult situation.   He was of course happy to have found his biological parents and blood related siblings but, he felt much closer to his previous parents, siblings and relatives than the present ones. "Yes, I put the interests of my childhood mother, ahead of the interests of my biological parents." He went on talking to himself, "how could I do differently?   How could I have left the slightest chance of disclosure of the fact to that wonderful human?   She would have had the most intolerable grief if she had realized that actually her son did die in her own arms so long ago and the son whom she brought up as her own was not hers."   He then began addressing them all, without noticing that, what he was about to say did not follow the topic that they were engaged in conversation.

"I hope you appreciate that I had to keep this secret to my-self. It was not that I didn't trust you but, I just could not afford creating slightest probability of accidental disclosure to any-one outside this family that, could reach to my Azeri mother's ears."

"Of course we appreciate," said Kathrine, "in fact grandma and mom praised you for that."

"Having brought up in another country and culture," he added, "I naturally have some romantic attachments and feel-ings about that land and people. I will continue to go and visit them and indeed there is no reason why they should know what I know now.   In fact, I rather my siblings over there continue regarding me as their genuine brother and the relatives to think of me as they have always done."

"Absolutely," said mother, "they are our cousins anyway. They're not strangers and I too would love to go and see them sometimes."

"I will do some teachings and surgical procedures there once or twice a year. They are very short of this speciality that I am being trained for. Indeed I owe that nation a lot and perhaps by some elective surgeries, teachings and charity activities I could compensate my debts to them."

"It is an excellent idea," said the father, "and you could com-bine visiting the relatives with teaching and the type of service you have in mind."What the son had not told them was that, after the funeral of mother, he talked to his siblings and dis-inherited himself from what mother had left for them, which was in fact quite substantial. Following his suggestion they all agreed to give one of the houses to the loyal servants of mother who were old couple.Once this done, he requested from couple, to allow him using one of the bedrooms whenever he returns there. The old couple agreed whole heartedly while tears falling from their eyes. They loved him and knew how much the lady loved her eldest son. He also contacted the medical school and offered teaching free of charge that they accepted with utmost delight. It was scheduled for twice a year and each time for two weeks, during which he would also do some elective surgeries. He asked one of the brothers to register and set up a charity organisation and run it personally.   He suggested that all the money which he would earn from doing surgical operations should go straight into that charity and the sum should be spent for education of children from poor families.   That night; he did not say anything about details of all these preparations to his parents, except for briefly informing them that he will regularly go to that country for teaching and doing some surgi-cal operations.   However, there were other subjects to inform them of, for which he was rather uncertain and did not know how they will react.   But he had made his mind about those issues too and had to let them know.

"We have to face with this odd reality that; I was brought up with different name, within a community and family with different religion from yours. As I only believe in God and have no religion that is not going to be a problem. But the name is an issue, which I had to make my mind about. Considering every-thing; I've decided to live the rest of my life with the same first and surnames. Father, I do hope that you would allow me to do so."

"I would have been happier," answered the father almost in tears, "if you had changed it to our family name but I can under-stand why you have decided otherwise."

"I am sorry father, but this is not disrespect to you. Every-one knows me with this name and I want to be the same person. Of course there are difficulties too." He said so and rather uncomfortably put his head down and remained silent. Kathrine interfered to help him by saying; "What is important is that God has returned your son and our dear brother to us. The name makes no difference."

"That is right." said mother, "I can't thank God enough." But grandmother reminded them that her husband had a lot of trouble because of his foreign name.

"Regrettably we have not been able to get rid of racism in this country," said David, "therefore anyone with different name or religion is considered an alien, a foreigner and an outsider no matter whether he was born here or how long has lived in this country." Father appeared gloomy and in deep thoughts and miracle son himself not at ease, felt sorry for him. He then referring to remarks of grandma and David said: "I have lived with that racism and hatred for many years. It is a shame that most people are racist. Strangely, in my childhood country, people love foreigners and are so hospitable and kind to them."

"I am sure you have considered everything," said the father, "I respect your decision my son; even though I hoped that like David you too would carry my name to the next generation."

"The celebration will continue," said David, "cheer up father." And so, the festive went on but rather less energetically. "I should have left it for some other time." said the elder brother inside. "I must encourage David to produce as many sons as he can to satisfy our father." He smiled to his thoughts and kept quiet for some time before joining the conversation again. It was wonderful to see after years of grievance, regret and self-blame, mother and grandmother were enjoying every minute of the celebration more than anyone else. And they all had the most memorable long weekend.

*

Few days later, Kathrine came to his apartment, affectionately hugged and kissed him then said, "I love you more than when you were my cousin and I am very proud of you."

"You love me more now because you know that I'm your brother but I love you a much as I used to because I knew you were my sister."

"Did you know even before the blood test?"

"I almost did because there were too many coincidence and chance to digest. I mean my mother's story, same location in two stories, my exact age, which of course you didn't know yet and the incredible resemblance could not be all mere coincidence."

"If I had not seen and known that admirable childhood mother of yours, I would have been very crossed with you for not telling me the truth. But I admit that you had every right to protect her and put her interest ahead of anyone else. As grandma said; it would be a great shame if we were the cause for her grief."

"Thank you for understanding. You said you are proud of me but why? What have I done to deserve it? "

"Because in most of the meetings and conferences that I attend, I hear they speak of you highly. You don't talk about your achievements. I would if I were you; to make mom and dad happy and proud. Once I talked to the professor you work with, and he told everything about you from the days you were a medical student until now. He warmly congratulated me when I said you were my cousin. I wished I knew you are my brother then; to be even more proud telling him so. Why don't you say anything about the honour degrees you have or, about your researches and articles? Why don't you say that, before even completing your training, they have offered you a consultant post in professor's department, and he believes that, you should succeed him as professor of neurosurgery when he retires?" She said it all with the utmost enthusiasm and emotion and her brother listened   in silence and politely although he wished to stop her praising.   Once there was a pause he kissed her and said; "My dear sister, they have exaggerated. Don't listen to them."

"I know about your researches and have read all of your ar-

185

ticles. I also know that you are now regarded as one of the best neurosurgeons in the country, even before finishing the years set aside for training. Stop being modest please."

"Okay they have offered me the post that is true. I will inform father and mother. Are you happy now?" She hugged him and said, "I will tell them everything myself." Kathrine informed her parents and brother that blood test confirms miracle son is their son and their brother. Once again grandmother boasted about her first impression and the very fact that she had no doubt about him being her grandson from the moment she saw the young man walking away from the car.

"When he apologised and walked away from the car," she said "I almost saw my husband again; apologising for blocking my way into the shop and walking away."

"I had a strange feeling," said the mother, "when I first hugged him as a cousin. I thought my son was in my arms."

"Mother's feeling is mysterious not only in humans but in animals' too." said the father, "I must admit that, after the initial shock of extreme likeness and hoping that grandma was right in her feelings, I accepted that the relationship with his mother explains the resemblance. Suspicion went on of course but I only became certain, when he said him-self and it was only then that I thought we did not need any more test. Well, that is what he wanted. Thank you for doing that Katherine." Miracle son was not present at that gathering and so, Kathrine took the opportunity and emotionally and proudly talked about her brother's accomplishments and how highly they talk about him in the hospitals that he works or in professional meetings and how much he is respected in the medical societies. These information made the parents very proud and happy which was what she wanted. Kathrine left the news of him being offered a consultant post and prospect of becoming a professor later on, to her brother to disclose. They had already informed the uncles in in USA and Germany, who were waiting for confirmation to come and see him. This was a rare occasion for reunion and they were all excited about it. The uncles came to visit their mother, sister and the rest of family but in particular to see their nephew; whom they never thought they would see him alive after being kidnapped and being presumed murdered, more than three decades ago. They were delighted and proud to see such an accomplished nephew who was highly regarded in United Kingdom. They donated five million pounds to his charity to astonishment and joy of the miracle son who said, "This is indeed very generous. It's well beyond my expectations. This money will certainly help our charity foundation to educate and train thousands of children from disadvantaged families to become scientist, medical professional, paramedics, engineer, lawyer and teacher for those kind and caring people whom I will never forget." And that is what was done and he even managed to bring several young doctors to be trained in various sub-specialities, which never existed in his childhood country.

*

Thereafter normal, routine and happy family life continued. Kathrine first and then David got married and very soon, grandchildren were produced to the pride and delight of parents. The older brother successfully achieved his ambition of visiting the land where he was brought up, visiting his brothers or relatives, teaching in the medical school or seminars and doing some elective surgeries there. A couple of years after regular visits to his beloved land he married a distant relative and the whole family went for his wedding in that country. They all retuned together, bringing the bride with them who had already learnt English in preparation for living in the United Kingdom. Miracle son had to tell the full story to his wife but advised her not to tell to anyone at native country.

Grandmother died at the age of ninety four. Thank God she achieved her desire of seeing great-grandchildren including miracle son's children. And as he had already documented and announced he did not accept any share from grandmother's inheritance either.

The end

Mohama is pen name of the author. Other books from the same author are;

1- Intelectuals of Cafe Naderi; was published by AuthorHouse. It has now been revised, edited and will be republished with different title "In searching God".

2- Agony of deniz; published by KDP.

Printed in Poland
by Amazon Fulfillment
Poland Sp. z o.o., Wrocław

62367390R00107